HE

TALL MAN'S WOMAN

TALL MAN'S WOMAN

by

Jake Douglas

Dales Large Print Books
Long Preston, North Yorkshire,
BD23 4ND, England.

British Library Cataloguing in Publication Data.

Douglas, Jake
    Tall man's woman.

A catalogue record of this book is
available from the British Library

ISBN   1-84262-230-7 pbk

First published in Great Britain in 2002 by Robert Hale Limited

Published in Large Print 2003 by arrangement with
Robert Hale Limited

Dales Large Print is an imprint of Library Magna Books Ltd.

Printed and bound in Great Britain by
T.J. (International) Ltd., Cornwall, PL28 8RW

PROLOGUE

The Town Tamer

They used to be friends.

First met when they ran away from their respective homes, tried to steal the same Indian canoe hidden in the reeds along the banks of the Wind River. They fought over it, scuffling and splashing, drew the attention of the Indian owner. Then they jumped aboard, grabbed paddles and clumsily nosed out into midstream with arrows zipping into the water all around them.

After they were out of range and their hearts had stopped hammering against their ribs, they had looked at each other; one of them grinned, then the other, and soon they were both laughing. When they had recovered they shook hands.

That handshake led them into years of wild trails, and more gunsmoke than they needed, and eventually saw them fighting side by side in the War on behalf of the Union.

Wounds and one of them being taken prisoner by the Rebs separated them and it was years later when they met once more and continued their friendship, riding the cattle trails and bending the law once in a while. It was all good fun – and then *she* came between them and afterwards, nursing their wounds from the fight, they rode down their own trails...

Nothing settled between them, they parted with a simmering hostility that boded ill if they ever met again.

Now they were face to face – in the dusty streets of Wichita, one riding at the head of a bunch of dirty, eager-for-hell-raising trail hands, the other standing in the middle of the street, holding up one hand, using the other to pull aside his vest so they could see the lawman's star.

The trail men reined down and their beard-shagged leader leaned forward in the saddle, thumbed back his hat, squinting.

'Well, I'll be dogged!' He turned to look at his wild bunch. 'Hey, fellers, we got us a real big sheriff here! See how tall he is? See that six-gun and the way he wears it? This is the one they call Town-Tamer – kicked the butts of trail men in Dodge, Abilene and a dozen other places. Now, I might be mistook, but I don't think I am – No, I reckon he's gonna give us a lecture, tell us to behave like good li'l boys while we're here or he'll slap our wrists and ask us to leave town!'

The rough trail-hands laughed but the sheriff's hard, weathered face didn't change.

'No slap on the wrists, boys. You kick over the traces and I'll slap you in jail. You'll be fined. *Then* I'll run you outta town.' The hard grey eyes swung to the trail boss. 'No lecture, Bill. Just have yourselves a good time but stay within the town ordinance.'

'Hell, make up your mind, big man!' Bill said, getting another laugh. 'Can't have a good time *and* stick to your lousy ordin-ance!'

'Give it your best shot,' advised the law-man.

He turned abruptly and walked back to his office, closing the door behind him.

Bill grinned crookedly over his shoulder at his men. 'Boys, I dunno about you, but I see that as a kinda challenge! What you say?'

With a chorus of wild wolf-calls they spurred forward in a group and thundered down Main, scattering the townsfolk and disrupting the wagon traffic, making straight for the nearest saloon...

The sheriff watched from a window, shook

his head slowly.

'Damn you, Bill! I knew you'd do it! You're gonna give me a hard time, you son of a bitch, just like you did with Holly! I tried once to make allowance for that bullet you took in the head at Gettysburg, but I ain't about to do it again.'

He watched as they dismounted and stormed through the batwings, jostling folk roughly aside. He swore softly, looked towards the closed doors of the cupboard beside his desk, stared a spell, ran a tongue over his lips. Then he swore again, strode across, yanked the door open and reached inside.

He brought out a bottle of rye whiskey, hesitated briefly, then tugged the cork loose with his teeth, spat it out, and tilted the neck against his mouth...

By sundown he was a mite unsteady on his feet, his head ringing with the shouts of the trail men, the sounds of breaking glass, splintering wood, the excited roaring of a crowd watching a brawl.

But after the first gunshots, he knew he couldn't avoid it any longer.

He checked his six-gun, dropping a cartridge, but he fumbled it back into the cylinder, slid the gun into its holster, and set his hat on his head – crookedly, but he didn't notice. He wiped the back of his hand across his dry lips and headed out on to Main. He walked down the middle of the street, weaving some, seeing folk on the walks watching him closely.

''Bout time you did somethin' about them trail boys, Sheriff!' called someone from the shadows and several other voices backed up the man.

The lawman waved casually, set his feet wide in the dust outside the saloon where all the racket was coming from, and called loudly,

'Bill Rankin! I want you out here right now! You hear me? Bill Rankin! Get out here!'

Bill came, backed by four or five of his drunken trail-men. All tended to stand close together so they could gain a mite of support from each other. Bill held a whiskey bottle by the neck. His face showed he had been in a fight – or two – blood dripping from a cut above his right eye.

'You called, big man?' he slurred.

'Get your crew together and hightail it outta town.'

'Ooooooh! He do sound pissed, don' he!' Rankin said, half-laughing, turning to look at his men.

They all chorused *'Oaaaaaoaaaohhh! He sure do, Bill!'*

Rankin grinned owlishly at the lawman. 'Trouble is, big man, I don' think we is quite ready to go.'

'You are.'

Rankin nodded solemnly. 'Yeah, he's pissed, all right. Seen him like this once before, long time ago. You recollect, big man? There was this – *lady* – name of Holly, weren't it…?'

'Get your men and go, Bill.' The sheriff's voice was quite clear now – although he swayed a little, right hand just a shade closer to his gun-butt.

Rankin was suddenly sober, his face scowling. 'What you gonna do? Draw on me?'

'Only if you're stupid enough to make the first move.'

'Oh? You mean like this?'

It took the lawman by surprise. He didn't think Bill Rankin's hate would still be at killing level, figured he was just showing off in front of his crew. But Bill *did* aim to kill him it seemed. Bill dropped the bottle and his men jostled each other to get out of the way when he shouted *'Gimme room!'* and slapped a hand against his gun-butt.

The sheriff reacted instinctively. His Colt palmed up smoothly, blurred in the half-light of sundown shadows, and the single shot crashed loud and final through the streets of Wichita.

Bill Rankin fell, a bullet shattering his heart.

The sheriff's face didn't change but when he holstered the smoking gun, his shoulders kind of sagged.

1

The Boss

Ross watched from the rim of the small canyon as the men below drove in the bunch of mavericks. They had rounded them up over the last couple of weeks, he reckoned, stashed them in a box canyon where they had built a fence across the entrance while they went back to gather more.

Now they were driving them into this hidden canyon he had long searched for, with its rough, weathered lean-to behind the line of piñons. What was more important were the remains of several camp-fires that he had discovered, and a set of crude running-irons – plus one well-made branding-iron in the form of a Broken Circle D.

There was no such brand within a hundred miles of here and it was not in the brand registration book, a copy of which he had with his gear back at the ranch.

It meant only one thing: these men were rounding up mavericks wherever they found them – and he knew damn well no boundary line would keep them from crossing on to neighbouring property.

Which amounted to rustling, even if the calves, or yearlings in some cases, as yet wore no brand.

But when they left this hidden canyon, which he had discovered only after long weeks of searching, he knew they would be branded Broken Circle D and whoever laid claim to them at the selling point would pocket the money.

Which meant Thistle was being robbed blind – by some of its own crew.

Well, he would have the absolute proof very shortly, he figured, moving warily around the rim so that he could get a better view down into the part behind the row of piñons.

They had a smokeless fire going now; he had suspected as much for, while there was no smoke to see, there had been a couple of distortions of the rising hot air, which he had caught out of the corner of his eye. Now he recognized the man tending the fire, stirring the heap of glowing coals with the branding iron. It was Kiley, a grubby, sweat-smelling man who seemed almost friendless amongst the ten-man crew of Thistle.

But he was greeted brightly enough by the two men driving the snorting, bawling mavericks into the prepared holding pen. They had built a chute, too, leading out of the pen to within a few feet of the fire. Someone had used his brains and made a lodge-pole frame where the maverick could be stretched out and held in position by a kind of gate hinged to the top of the frame while the branding-iron was applied and, he suspected, an identifying nick made in the ear.

That would allay any lingering suspicions a buyer might have: rustlers usually didn't take the time to make ear-notches. But these men were apparently working in complete safety here in the back-blocks of the huge Thistle spread.

He had his dog-eared notebook with him and made notes, identifying the two riders as Stew Hagen and Race Satterfield. He shook his head slowly: as Dysart, the Thistle's owner, had suspected, it was all being done from the inside. Well, it wouldn't last much longer, not now that he had seen this with his own eyes. All he had to do was...

'Pretty neat set-up, huh?'

The tall, lean man sprawled on the rim,

spun violently on to his back, dropping his notebook and clumsily reaching towards his six-gun butt. But he froze when he saw the saddle carbine covering him, the hammer back, the owner's gnarled finger curled around the trigger.

It was another of the cowhands, the one he thought they called Wrango...

'Point that gun somewhere else, Wrango!' he snapped, cursing inwardly because his mouth was so dry with fear that the words kind of *squeaked* out.

'Might do that – later. Right now, it's aimed at you so you better do like I say – *Boss!*'

'If you're mixed up in this, Wrango, nothing will save you, I promise you!'

'Aw, now why you talkin' like that? I ain't threatened you or nothin'. Look, stand up. No, no, I ain't gonna do nothin' to you – Just stand up. *Now!*'

The manager of Thistle stood slowly, careful to keep his hands well away from his gun butt. Wrango, a solid man of stocky build, grinned tightly.

'See? You're OK. And you'll stay that way long as you do what you're told. We've been a long time settin' things up so you'll savvy we ain't just gonna toss it all away. Not when we got a ready market waitin'. But you're only manager here. Not like they was your own mavericks. I ain't sure about the rest but I kinda like you. You treated us all pretty good, so I figure it's worth goin' down there and talkin' with the others. See if they'll cut you in – then you won't be able to do nothin' but go along with the deal, OK?'

He could see the tall man thinking about it, thinking about how it would be best to agree, hoping for a chance to break free before he got down to the others in the hidden canyon.

'We-ell – like you say, they ain't my mavericks. I'm willing to listen to a deal. Not promising anything, but...'

'That's OK. We'll still have the upper hand whatever you say. Hey, look! You see how that clampin' frame works? Man, the boss sure knew what he was doin' when he built that!'

The lean man snapped his head up. 'You're not the leader?'

Wrango scoffed. 'Not me! I don't have enough brains for that, but – *look!* See how blame easy it is to brand one of them critters even when they want to act up...?'

The tall man turned to look and suddenly

the butt of the carbine smashed between his shoulders; his eyes flew wide and his mouth opened as he staggered forward – and his scrabbling boot stepped out into space.

'Go on down an' say howdy!'

Wrango watched him fall, screaming all the way down.

'I ain't takin' no orders from no woman!'

'Me, neither!'

'No one said you have to.'

'Shoot, Abe, if she's the new manager's wife, she'll be bossin' us all around! Nope, I'm quittin'! Never had no use for a bossy woman, never had!'

'I'm goin' with you, Stew!'

'Neither of you is goin' anywhere. Now just set down and shut up and I'll put you in the picture, OK?'

The two cowhands stiffened at his tone.

Abe McKinley was the foreman of Thistle, and there wasn't a bigger man in the whole of the Bitterroot country. He stood six feet seven and he was built like a gladiator of old, smooth rippling muscles, a rifle-butt brown skin – he worked on a sun tan, stripping to the waist whenever he could out doors – jet black hair with tight curls, a face like those on statues of Greek gods. His favourite trick was to pick up the anvil in the blacksmith's shop and lift it over his head ten times in a row – then hurl it several yards.

Right afterwards he would snap a vesta into flame with a thumbnail, hold it steady so it was obvious his hands weren't even shaking with effort, then, pushing his arm out as far as it would go, he would blow it out with a single breath.

He was a show-off, was Abe McKinley, and some said he 'kissed himself goodnight' – but not out loud. In fact, most men with even an ounce of sense bent over backwards to applaud McKinley. The few who had been stupid enough to sass him or even try to outdraw him were now either resting peacefully in some windswept boot hill or using crutches to get around, a constant reminder of opening their mouth at the wrong time, to the wrong man.

Now – in the ranch house's untidy parlour – McKinley had moved into the main house after the body of the manager was found jammed amongst the rocks of Puma Rapids in the hard-flowing Sioux River a few weeks back – McKinley watched as the men sat down at his command. He leaned his slim hips against the big, scarred table and folded his arms. He held a dog-eared yellow form in his big right hand and glanced at it briefly, reading in his deep voice.

New Manager arriving 27th. Mr and Mrs Cody Travis. Make them welcome. See that they're met and shown every courtesy. These folk are good friends of mine.

McKinley paused and looked at his men. 'Signed by Jock Dysart himself – But he says *manager*, no "s".

'The wife's just tagging along is my guess. Might make a nuisance of herself trying to spruce up the place, but I'll see she stays outta everyone's hair...' His brown eyes suddenly hardened as he flicked them from one man to the other. 'Give him a chance, see how he shapes.'

'And if he don't?' asked Stew Hagen, a man with a wide, flat face and high cheekbones, giving him an oriental look.

'That's for Dysart to worry about. He hired him. If they get here by the 27th I want 'em to find the place in pretty good shape and you see the men show 'em some respect. We don't want complaints about us finding their way back to the owner. That damn Scotsman is bone-headed enough to

21

fire the lot of us if he takes the notion.'

'I dunno, Abe, I'm still not keen about a woman comin' in here.'

'Stew, ain't you figured out yet that it don't matter a spit into the wind what *you* like or don't?'

Hagen looked suddenly wary. Like everyone else, he didn't want to get on the wrong side of Abe McKinley.

'Well, it's just that I had enough of ranchers' wives interfering when I worked the Red River spreads. Had to take a bath every Saturday, no work after midday Sunday, then git cleaned up in decent clothes, hair plastered down with water or axle grease, even your boots polished! Then we had to sing hymns and say grace before eatin'. An' them women was *every-damn-where!* Hear you cuss and they take a dollar outta your pay. See you kick a hoss in the slats that's just stomped on your foot and get the old man to give you a tongue-lashin', make you muck-out the stables, curry-comb the goddamn bronc for a week – and then they upset the cook, makin' him wash his hands, givin' him recipes they reckoned was good for us – lousy grub with no spices or salt! I tell you, I quit that country lickety-split.'

The other man, Kiley, squirmed uncomfortably. 'Hell, Abe, I hope it ain't gonna be that way when she comes!'

'It won't be,' the foreman said confidently. 'But you spread the word with the boys – go easy, ride the punches a spell until we get the feel of 'em. An' if they don't measure up the way we want 'em, why, *then* we'll make our move and show 'em how *we* want the place run. They'll soon figure they can't get nowhere without us.'

Kiley looked a little easier but Hagen said slowly, looking up into Big Abe's handsome face:

'You said *if* they arrive on the 27th... You mean *when?*'

McKinley smiled crookedly, shaking his head. 'Meant what I said. They're newly-weds. On their honeymoon. Would you hurry to start work on a place like this?'

'Aw, shoot!' Kiley spat. 'Not just friends of that damn Limey, but goddamn greenhorns to boot!'

Stew Hagen pursed his lips. 'Well, mebbe that ain't so bad. We can train 'em to do what *we* want 'em to do.'

He looked to Abe McKinley for reassurance but the big man said, flatly,

'Or maybe that's just what we're meant to think.'

It took a couple of minutes for the two cowhands to figure out what the ramrod was getting at.

And when they did, their grimy faces lost most of their colour.

2

Greenhorns

The riverboat hooted as it rounded the moonlit bend of the wide river, steam blasting across the stars like a ghostly exclamation mark.

Standing in the shadows of the look-out deck above him, Cody Travis drew on his long cheroot and watched the big stern paddle-wheel churn the river into foam, the long, hardwood blades glistening as they turned. The deck beneath his feet trembled with the throb of the big steam engines and he could just detect a squeak in one of the pushrod bearings somewhere down in the bowels of the riverboat.

He watched the night and the dark shore, occasionally broken by the dim yellow of lights in settlers' lonely cabins or, once, a camp-fire that might have meant either Indians or a trapper. He touched his vest pocket and felt the bulge of the gold coins he had just won in the gambling saloon below. Seventy-seven dollars. Unbelievable. Not like his usual run of luck – but then lately, his 'luck' had taken a different turn from what it had been the last couple of years. Or should that be *most of his life...?*

Well, all that time he had been living in the nightmare-shot darkness he had no one to blame but himself. It had been his choice and he had sunk about as low as a man could before – something – had allowed him a glimpse of a distant bright light. Its meaning had escaped him, of course, but one time when there had been no more booze available, while he waited for the horror of withdrawal, something had gone *click!* in his brain and he had seemed to be looking down at himself from a point several feet in the air. He was sprawled amidst the trash of some strange, stridden alley filthy, half-starved – hell, half-*loco!* – sick in both mind and body, about ten steps from the grave.

The shock had almost literally stopped his heart.

That had been a *real* bad time, real bad.

Somehow he had made it through and when he had come back to reality, to *life*, he had glimpsed the light again as he lay in a bed with clean sheets and Abby bending over him, smiling, wiping his gaunt, wild-eyed face with a damp cloth. Her quiet voice soothed him, allayed his fears.

'You can come back to us now, Mr Travis. The worst is over. You'll have plenty of help from now on...'

And he did. Mostly from Abigail Roth.

He smiled at the dark river, at the memory. It was a time he would never forget, a time of returning to a normal life where there was real happiness, not just a liquor-induced euphoria that too often turned to raging horror before the onset of the oblivion he sought.

It was a long journey back and he owed much to the sanitarium doctors, but mostly to Abby, a hell of a lot to her...

She would be waiting for him now in their cabin on B Deck and he pictured the way her face would light up when he told her he had won at faro...

Then they came at him, one from either side, moving like pieces of the darkness itself under the look-out deck.

He had good peripheral vision and although he was looking at the river, he saw them both, closing in fast, aiming to put him out of action pronto. Then they would rifle his pockets and be gone in seconds. Maybe they'd throw his unconscious body over the rail first...

These thoughts flashed through his mind. Then his left hand holding the cheroot stabbed out at the man closing from that side, and he felt flesh cringe as the glowing tip ground into it. There was a stink of burning meat just before the man howled and clapped both hands to his face, swaying wildly to one side, moaning as he crashed into the rail.

Travis ducked as the one on the right swung his short billy. He heard the hardwood smash into the wall behind his head. He came up from a low crouch, twisting his right hand into the man's groin, actually lifting the attacker clear of the deck. The man gave a strangled scream as his genitals mashed and Travis bared his teeth, clapped his other hand to the throat and ran the attacker backwards along the deck. The stern rail caught him low in the back and he arched over, thrashing wildly as wide, pain-filled eyes saw the whirring blades of the paddle-wheel, river water drenching him. His gagging scream was lost in the thrashing of the water as he fell, tangled briefly in the blades and then his body was ploughed under.

By now his companion had recovered

enough to close with Travis. He caught him as he turned from the rail and punched him in the face, twice. Travis's head snapped back and he tasted blood. One eye began to fill and he wrenched his head aside as a third blow sliced towards him. He was too slow. It took him on the ear; his head rang and his sense of balance was lost enough to throw him sideways into the rail.

The robber grunted in satisfaction and, his face burning from the cheroot, feeding his anger, ran at Travis, reaching for him, aiming to throw him into the river. Cody Travis ducked low, moved in a crouch to one side and stepped forward, twisting as he straightened. The move put him behind the attacker and he grabbed the back of the man's head, feeling greasy hair under his fingers. He smashed the ugly face into the upright, fluted-metal post supporting the look-out deck. Bone crunched and blood sprayed. Hurt, the man staggered back and Travis lowered his shoulder as he spread a hand across the other's chest and shoved.

The man must have already been unconscious because he didn't make a sound as he plunged into the dark river.

'What's wrong with your face?'

Travis swore softly to himself as he closed the door behind him. He thought she would be in bed, reading. But Abby was on the sofa in the cabin's small sitting-room, a cup of coffee in her hand, frowning as he turned, holding a white kerchief to the cut above his right eye. He forced a smile.

'Walked slap into a door someone left open on the rear deck,' he lied, taking the cloth away and looking at the blood. 'It's not much.'

But she was there in front of him now, forcing down his hand as he raised the kerchief towards his face again. She frowned as she examined the cut.

'It's split open. It could use a stitch or two.'

'It's not that bad, Abby. I'll just wash up and–'

'I'm the nurse, remember?' She said it with a smile but she was emphatic, and poured water from a china jug into a bowl and set to work. 'It'll need drawing together with tape. Lucky I have some in my kit.'

As she started to move away, he took her arm, spun her back against him and kissed her on the mouth. 'Lucky *I* have *you!*'

She drew back and her face was sober for a moment before she smiled. He watched with pleasure, as always, as her eyes crinkled – they did it every time she smiled. She pushed a hand gently against his chest.

'We'd better try and stop that bleeding.'

He watched her walk into the bedroom, her body briefly outlined through the thin robe she was wearing. She was a fine-looking woman and he still couldn't believe his luck – *was that what it was? Really?* – at winning her heart. It had been like being caught up in a whirlwind after he had recovered at the mountain clinic and gained some control over his own life again. The day they discharged him, she was waiting at the gate, smiling, taking his arm.

'You can walk me into town, Cody. I have the afternoon off.'

That had been the start of other walks and meetings and eventually a courtship so swift and gratifying that he thought he must be dreaming when he found himself in the small church in the lazy Mississippi River town saying *'I do'*.

But just before that, something strange had happened, something he hadn't yet figured out: Abby had changed so much and so swiftly that, for a time, he had believed they would never make that walk down the aisle.

He'd found her in her room, hearing her

sobs as he entered silently, the small wedding-gift he had bought in his pocket, eager to see the pleasure light up her face when she opened it. Alarmed by the sounds of crying coming from her bedroom, he'd been even more alarmed to find the door locked.

He rapped the panel hard with his knuckles.

'Abby? What's wrong? Open up – I want to help you!'

But she hadn't opened the door for long minutes and when she had, she was dressed for travelling, a small valise in one hand, her reddened eyes now dry, her lovely face set in stiff sober lines. Her eyes were cool as they looked up into his.

'There's nothing you can do, Cody,' she told him with a cold edge to her voice he had never heard before. 'I – I've received some news and I have to – go away for a short time.'

Stunned, he blinked. 'What're you talking about? Our wedding day is Saturday! Just four days away!'

'I'm sorry. Put it off. I'll be back as soon as I can, Cody. I promise!'

She stood on tiptoe and kissed him lightly on the mouth. Then she spun away as he tried to grasp her, held up a hand in front of his face.

'Don't try to stop me, Cody! Or you'll never see me again!'

Bewildered, heart pounding, he had watched her hurry away to the railroad depot, just in time to board the northbound train.

It was two weeks before she returned and she was different. Every bit as beautiful, but it was a sober beauty now; she didn't smile anywhere near so much as previously. She never mentioned why she had left or where she had been and he had never asked; he was just happy to have her back.

They were married two days later, his head all a-swirl, wondering whether after all this was really only some alcohol-induced dream...

Then, shortly after the wedding, he was offered this job as manager of a Montana cattle ranch. Abby told him that the doctor she used to work for, the one who had treated Travis in the clinic, knew the Scotsman who owned the ranch and had recommended Cody for the job.

Puzzled, yet pleased, he answered many questions about his past, most of them truthfully enough, wondering why Dysart kept coming back to his days as a lawman.

Hell, he had only packed a star for less than a year, part-time mostly, but the rancher wanted to know all the details. He hadn't told him everything, just enough to show himself in as good a light as possible. He not only wanted this job, he *needed* it.

Of course, he had stretched the truth a mite as far as his claims for experience in managing ranches went – he'd been more of a trail man than a ranch hand – but he knew cattle and felt confident that he could handle the job of running the Thistle spread. As long as Abby was at his side, he felt he could handle anything life threw his way... But would she want to go way out to the Bitter-root country, far from towns and what passed for civilization?

He needn't have worried. Abby didn't hesitate when he told her the job was his if he wanted it.

'Oh, take it Cody! It sounds like it would be a wonderful experience! I'd love to help run a ranch!'

So he had told Dysart he'd take the job and now they were on their way to the Thistle ranch.

After she had taped up his cut eyebrow neatly, she seemed about to speak but he slid his arms around her waist and silenced her with a brief kiss, smiling down at her.

'I won almost eighty dollars at faro and I want to celebrate. How about a late supper with all the trimmings?'

She smiled her agreement, even if a mite bewildered by the sudden switch and then lifted his shirt-front which she had been toying with. She looked up into his eyes. 'That door you ran into must've been splintered. You've torn your shirt.'

He laughed. 'So I'll buy a new one! I can afford it!'

'Cody – have you been in a fight? Did someone try to rob you of your winnings?'

His face straightened and then he smiled again. 'You've got some imagination, Abby! I told you: I – walked – into – a – door!'

She nodded, and said she would go and change, but in her job as a nurse, she had seen too many split eyebrows caused by hard knuckles not to be able to recognize such a wound.

She said no more to him but she hated it when he lied to her.

Hated it even more than when she had to lie to him.

The riverboat took them as far as Casper,

Wyoming, and then they caught a train to end-of-track at Lander in the foothills of the Wind River range. It was a lot colder up here than where they had come from, still early spring, but a mighty cold one for blood as thin as theirs.

They went by stage over the mountains and through the stunning Teton country with its snow-capped peaks and scattered settlers, turning north to the newly opened Yellowstone National Park.

Cody Travis, a man who had seen almost all of the United States was awed by the park's beauty and the amount of wildlife: grizzly bears, buffalo in their thousands, moose, elk, mountain sheep and goats, rivers so full of fish that they leapt high into the air, sunlight flashing from their arcing bodies. The forests were alive with birds and their various songs. The air was sweet with scents of the forest.

'Must be a piece of heaven that fell to earth,' he allowed to Abby and she turned slowly, startling him when he saw her eyes were full of tears. He slid an arm around her shoulders. 'Yeah – it is kind of – overwhelming, ain't it?'

She merely nodded, but he felt there was a tension in her and that tight knot began to form in his belly again as it had when she had gone away before the wedding. But she dabbed at her eyes and smiled.

'It – it's wonderful, Cody – wonderful.'

That almost satisfied him, but he glimpsed her teeth tugging at her lower lip, a habit he'd noticed she had when she was upset and trying not to show it.

Goddamnit! What the hell was wrong!

'I knew a park ranger from here once. We were very close, but – he's dead now.'

That likely explained her sombre mood, Cody thought, realizing just how little he really knew about her.

Then she brightened – he noticed she made a special effort – and the rest of the ride through the park was more pleasurable for both, as they gawked and pointed to this or that like a couple of greenhorns on their first trip into the wilderness.

They crossed into Idaho briefly and then swung up to Montana, into the Bitterroot country. Their destination was Hap Hawkins Creek way station where they would be met by someone who would take them out to Thistle.

'Won't be long now, Abby,' he said, unable to hide the edge of excitement in his voice.

She smiled and it wavered a little at the

edges, but then spread wide again, the skin around her eyes crinkling. She laid a hand gently on his as they waited for their guide.

'No, Cody – not long now.'

Was there a hint of strain in her words?

3

'Welcome To Thistle!'

Abe McKinley sent Wrango to meet them at Hap Hawkins Creek way station.

There was no particular reason for choosing Wrango except he was a good buckboard driver and knew the long trail well. He greeted the Travises with a handshake for Cody and a tip of his battered hat and a half-smile for Abby.

'Glad you folks made it OK,' he said, trying not to show his surprise at the cases and carpetbags the stage driver unloaded out of the Concord's boot and stacked in the weak sunlight. 'That all, ma'am?'

Wrango tried to keep the sarcasm out of his voice but failed just a little and Abby dropped her smile, nodding curtly. She didn't care for people who made sly remarks.

'Give you a hand to load it into the buckboard,' offered Travis, but as he made to move forward Abby held his arm. He looked down at her, puzzled.

'You're the *manager*, Cody,' she said in a low voice but loud enough for the sweating Wrango to hear. 'Wrango is the ranch hand. It's his job to load luggage, not yours.'

Cody Travis was a mite surprised at this attitude of Abby's and he caught the quick look Wrango threw her, but she tugged insistently and said, 'We've time for a cup of coffee before we go.'

'Well, now, ma'am,' spoke up Wrango, catching her words, 'I'd as lieve start as soon as we're loaded. We've a far piece to travel and the more miles we can make before dark the better.'

'I understand,' she told him coolly, 'but I have travelled several hundred miles and my throat is dry from the dust. I feel in need of some hot coffee and perhaps a cool wash if the agent's wife can oblige...'

Wrango glanced at Travis's blank face and figured he wasn't about to argue with the new boss's wife, so he merely nodded and climbed aboard the creaking buckboard, starting to arrange the luggage. A thistle was painted on each side-board.

'He could be right about making as much mileage as we can before dark, Abby. That sky looks kind of threatening out yonder.'

'We have time for coffee, Cody,' she said adamantly. He shrugged and they walked across to the station porch where the half-breed Indian agent and his fullblood wife waited.

At the night camp at the end of the second day's travel, Wrango said, 'Don't like the look of them clouds. See the green and purple tinge? Hail's comin' and we get it fifty-calibre size out here...'

'And what d'you plan to do about that?' Abby asked coolly. 'Now that we are fore-warned – that is if you are a good weather-prophet, of course.'

Travis couldn't understand her attitude, but he had the notion it was due to a tension that seemed to be gnawing at her and which he suspected was increasing the closer they got to journey's end.

'There's a cave in them hills that might be big enough for us and the hosses,' Wrango said curtly.

'The horses, too?' Abby asked, eyebrows raised. Wrango sighed but it was Travis who explained the horses could be badly injured by heavy hailstones. 'And without horses in this country, Abby, we won't last long. The odd Indian renegade still roams these hills.'

'Oh. Well, I'm afraid I'm your original greenhorn when it comes to travelling in the wilderness.'

But Wrango's forecast was wrong – although probably big hailstones did tear up the country a little more to the north. But the trio got heavy rain and were glad to shelter in the cave. The original campsite was washed away by flash flooding and Abby was displeased that one of her valises was now travelling part-way across Montana without her.

But she didn't fuss about it and soon was admiring the rain-clear countryside, sharper and more colourful after the night's deluge.

'The sky seems so big,' she said. '*Everything* seems so big and there's so much – emptiness. You never explained the vast emptiness to me, Cody.'

'Don't think you asked me much about the country, Abby,' he said slowly, looking closer at her. He saw her small frown, and then her cheeks flushed a little.

'Oh – well, it must've been someone else.'

Another two days and they were in Bitterroot country with the range of the same name appearing in the distance, hazy and saw-toothed. On a ridge they saw a group of six

Indians watching them and Abby grabbed Travis's arm tightly. Wrango saw and smiled crookedly.

'Don't worry none, ma'am. They won't bother us.' He reached back and slapped the left-hand sideboard, indicating the crudely painted thistle. 'They know better.'

Travis wondered exactly what that meant but didn't pursue it. Seemed the thistle was some kind of warning.

By mid-afternoon they caught their first glimpse of grazing cattle and Wrango told them they were Thistle cows.

'Thistle land goes clear back to the Bitter-roots themselves. Had a bad winter and this spring is colder'n usual. Grass is slow so we got cows scattered to hell-an'-gone, trying to make it last out till summer.' He pointed. 'House is over yonder rise – the big hog-back. Be there afore dark.'

'Thank goodness!' said Abby with feeling. 'I hope your cook will have hot water for my bath.'

'Ba...?' began Wrango, sounding sur-prised, and then cut the word and said, 'I 'spect he'll heat some for you if that's what you want, ma'am.'

'Of course he will,' she replied, smiling sweetly; there was not a doubt in her tone that the cook would do as he was told.

'I b'lieve the other manager drowned,' Travis said, uneasy about the woman and the way she was behaving: he had never seen this side of her before.

Wrango looked up sharply, taken off-guard by the sudden change of subject. 'Er – yeah – looked like he'd been ridin' along the river's edge near the rapids and the bank collapsed – the way that white water spews down there it can undercut a mile of bank in a couple of hours at times. Found him wedged in some rocks, banged around somethin' awful...'

'Who found him?'

Travis had been about to speak but the words died as he whipped his head around to stare at Abby. She had snapped her question and he saw her face was tight, pale under the trail grime.

'Was me, ma'am,' Wrango told her quietly. 'He'd been gonna meet me up in the canyon country but must've gotten lost on the way. I found his hoss, first, all wet and muddy, hurt from the river. I back-trailed and found Mr Ross after a deal of searchin'. Nice feller. We was all sorry to see him die that way.'

'You buried him on Thistle land?'

44

Funny question for Abby to ask, allowed Travis to himself, but Wrango answered mildly enough.

'Never mentioned any kin so we laid him to rest in the little boot hill we got...'

Abby seemed no longer interested, wheeled her mount and faked with her spurs. 'Let's hurry! The sooner I get that bath the better!'

She ran her mount down into the hollow between the hills and Travis spurred his grey after her. Wrango whipped up the buck-board team, his hard face thoughtful.

Kinda strange couple, he allowed. *The man don't even pack a gun. Woman's a looker but seems bossy and Travis seems content to let her have her way...*

Somehow Wrango didn't think that was a good thing. Still, Abe would know what to do.

There wasn't much that Big Abe Mc-Kinley couldn't handle.

They were both impressed with Abe Mc-Kinley's size and good looks. He gave Travis a bone-crushing handshake, taking the new manager unawares. But Cody composed his face and didn't allow any pain to show. Abe smiled crookedly as he released his hand and nodded a mite curtly to Abby, doffing

45

his hat so that the sun glinted off his raven-black curls.

'Welcome to Thistle,' he said in his deep voice. 'Hope you'll both be happy here. Look, I moved into the house after Ross was killed, haven't had time to get my gear out or tidy up properly...'

'Oh, well,' said Abby brightly, glancing up at the sky, the clouds edged in a riot of colour now the sun was sinking into the west, almost touching the knife-edges of the distant Bitterroots. 'There should be time before dark to get things in order. We'll leave you to it and just take a stroll around, meantime.'

McKinley's smile disappeared and his eyes narrowed but Abby had already dismissed him, taking her husband's arm. 'Let's have a look at the barn and the bunkhouse, Cody. And I'd like to see the cook-shack, too...'

Travis locked gazes with the sober-faced ramrod and gave him a crooked smile and a shrug of the shoulders, at the same time rocking his right hand, letting the man know he could expect no sympathy from him.

'See what I mean about the woman bein' bossy?' Wrango said out of the corner of his mouth, still offloading Abby's luggage.

'Get that damn mountain of stuff up on to

the porch and send Stew and Race up to lend a hand clearin' out my gear,' growled McKinley

Wrango nodded, amused and trying to hide it. It could have been an accident when Big Abe turned sharply and caused Wrango to drop the three valises he was struggling with, but the ramrod didn't stop to say 'sorry'. Wrango swore and bellowed for Stew Hagen and Race Satterfield until they reluctantly showed in the door of the bunkhouse and finally started slowly across the yard.

They nodded to the Travises and Cody stopped them, asked their names, introduced Abby and himself. The men mumbled 'howdys' and continued on towards the house.

In the big bunkhouse, untidy and smelling strongly enough of man-sweat and other male odours for Abby to put her perfumed kerchief against her nose, there were only two other cowhands – Kiley and the wrangler, Billy Jo Enderby. They started to leave but Abby stopped them, turned to Cody.

'This place is a pigsty, Cody, a hotbed of disease. Lord only knows what germs are breeding up in here – I think one of the priorities is to get it swamped out and all the bedding washed and aired.'

'We'll see what range chores are in progress, Abby,' Travis told her quietly and she frowned.

'Cody, I'm a nurse – or was until recently. I cannot abide living in filth or having someone else live in filth if I know filth exists. Good hygiene must take precedence over any so-called ranch chores ... can we get to the cookshack out of that door?'

She addressed the question to the bony wrangler and he nodded, sniffing, then pulled out a crumpled and dirty kerchief and blew his nose. Abby curled a lip disdainfully, striding towards the door. Travis followed slowly and Billy Jo made a low sound like a chicken clucking, winking at Kiley who scowled.

'Yeah – hen-pecked already and Abe says they only been married a couple weeks.'

Travis broke stride, hesitated, but didn't turn, followed his wife through the door into the cookshack – where she was already berating the one-legged cook over his lack of hygiene in preparing the evening meal...

'Gonna be a real fun-time if she's startin' out like this ten minutes after she's arrived,' allowed Stew Hagen in the house, gathering up some of McKinley's clothing.

Big Abe, stuffing some papers into a carton, turned to look at Stew, his expression taut. 'Have to give her a little leeway, I guess, till we see which way the wind's blowin'. But she ain't gonna run this place like no Sunday School.'

'Or a goddamn infirmary,' allowed Race Satterfield, overweight and already breathing hard and sweating harder from helping get the furniture back in its original position. 'I spent a month in one in Cheyenne once when I busted a leg – nearly drove me loco. "Wash your hands after goin' to the privy Mr Satterfield". "Lemme see your nails before you eat...". "You can't wear those longjohns! They're so dirty they can stand by themselves...".' Race shook his head slowly. 'I'll quit rather than go through that again.'

'No one's quittin',' said Big Abe heavily, staring out of the grimy window at the sundown-washed yard, seeing the Travises leaving the cookshack, the woman talking animatedly to Cody. 'Unless it's them two. It's about time I heard from Stedmann. Sent him a wire to find out what he could about this Travis. Till we know somethin' definite, we let 'em have their head for a spell. But if what I suspect is right, I aim to haul rein hard enough to break a couple of necks!'

Abe McKinley was going through his exercise routine the next morning when the Travises stepped out on to the porch. The big ramrod pretended not to see them but he added a little more style to his efforts, lifting the big anvil faster and trying to make it look as if he wasn't expending much energy. The muscles swelled under his sweat-sheened skin and stood out as if sculpted in marble.

Abby, as a nurse, was interested in the anatomical aspects of the man's performance and remarked to Cody that she had probably never seen a more perfect torso on any man.

He looked down at her sharply but she smiled crookedly and poked him lightly in the ribs.

'Now don't go getting jealous – it's purely a professional opinion.'

'Uh-huh. He sure is a sight though.'

'In love with himself,' she said shortly, then raised her voice a little. 'Mr McKinley – *Mr McKinley*. Can you come across for a moment?'

Travis frowned, wondering why she had called McKinley. The big man didn't seem too pleased at having to interrupt his routine and continued lifting the anvil several times before raising it high over his head, then tossing it as nonchalantly as possible – not even grunting with effort – several yards back towards the blacksmith's shop.

Most of the crew were watching from around the bunkhouse or outside the cookshack. They grinned and nudged each other as McKinley swaggered across, paused at the foot of the porch steps, took out a vesta, snapped it into flame with his thumbnail and then extinguished it at arm's length with one breath. He grinned.

'Like to keep fit.'

'Well, you certainly seem to be that,' allowed the woman. 'Mr McKinley, I thought you were asked to remove your belongings from the house last night.'

'Aw, yeah, I know what you're gettin' at. That bunk I rigged in the office and a couple chairs I moved up from the bunkhouse – comfortable ones. Never had time to do it last night...'

'You could have made time,' she told him. 'Anyway you'll find your furniture and the books you left and some clothes you neglected to take from behind the parlour door in a heap out in the back yard. I think one of your chairs suffered a little damage.'

McKinley was no longer smiling. He flicked his hard gaze from the woman to Travis. 'Weren't no need for that. I'd've got 'em out this mornin'.'

'Well, the job's already done,' Travis said flatly.

'Uh-huh. You want to read my reports I wrote while I was fillin' in after Ross got himself killed?'

'We'll have breakfast first,' Abby told him. 'If the men have eaten you can give them their chores and then wash up. We should be finished eating by that time.'

She gave him a quick, meaningless smile, took Travis's arm and turned back into the house. McKinley kept his face perfectly blank but scraped sweat-beads from his forehead with a curled finger and flicked them away with a disdainful motion, muttering:

'Uppity bitch! You need bringin' down a peg or so.'

Then, his good mood shattered, he began bawling orders to the men. The yard became a hive of activity for the next few minutes as horses were roped and saddled, tools were gathered and the men made their way to various parts of the ranch to do their chores.

McKinley washed his torso behind the cookshack, pulled on his workshirt, gathered his reports and made his way to the house.

Abby met him at the door, took the papers and told him he could wait in the bunkhouse or busy himself at something in the yard while they read through them.

'Maverick count seems to be down,' opined Cody Travis later, confronting Big Abe near the pump where the man had been fixing the handle and worn plunger.

McKinley glanced up, still working with a spanner on the gooseneck-seal nuts.

'Yeah, well, we ain't been too far back into the hills yet. Still a little snow up there. Was a bad winter and this spring ain't shaped up too well so far. Man can still freeze his ass off.'

'Mr Dysart gave me some projected figures which he reckoned ought to be fairly accurate. You're *way* down on them.'

Abe glanced up, his face showing his irritation. 'I just told you – snow's stopped us goin' way back in the hills where we're likely to find mavericks. The chore'll get done.'

'Yeah, it will, but not as long as you dilly-dally around because of a little cold weather. Get some men choosing mavericks tomorrow. And just how far back into the hills do you go, anyway?'

McKinley covered his rising anger swiftly, wariness creeping into his manner now.

'Quite a ways.'

'Well, watch the line with Horseshoe. Dysart said Anders has complained some of the mavericks on his range have found their way into Thistle's herds.'

'Sure, that's possible – I mean a maverick is a maverick, right? No brand. It belongs to whoever drops a rope on it.'

'Just watch that line and don't cross it. We don't need trouble with the neighbours.'

The ramrod shrugged. 'How tight you gonna run this place, you don't mind me askin'? I mean, I got my own way of doin' things and Dysart ain't complained to me about the way I operate so far...'

'I'll try not to cramp your style, but – he didn't automatically make you manager, though, when Ross was killed, did he?'

The big foreman stood up slowly, greasy spanner still in one hand. Travis noticed that the knuckles of the hand that grasped the tool were dead white.

'No, he didn't,' he said quietly

'You were expecting him to move you up to manager?'

'Figured he might. Like I said, we've returned some pretty good figures last couple of seasons.'

'Not as good as he'd like. Sure, a profit, but by this time, he'd reckoned on more.'

'So he put you in. You some kinda expert, huh?'

'I've worked with cows for years,' was all Travis said and McKinley felt a shaft of quickening interest.

Seemed to him, this new manager didn't really want to talk about how much he knew and how much he didn't – or how long it was since he'd last worked with cattle.

He decided to take a ride into Fort Hatfield when he could and see if anything had come back from Stedmann.

He didn't have to make the ride.

Sheriff Lew Birch came in around midday. He had a letter addressed to Abe and another for Abby Travis.

He was a medium-sized man, gone to fat a little now, although he had the look of a man who had once been fit enough. Birch was in his fifties, moved slowly and deliber- ately and, Travis thought, was maybe slowed down some by encroaching rheumatics. He had a worn, saggy kind of face, sported a longhorn moustache, yellow-brown from tobacco, beneath a nose with flared nostrils. But his eyes were what you noticed most.

Steel-grey, penetrating, they had the look of being able to spot a rider way out on the horizon without strain.

They were now studying Cody Travis and the ranch manager felt a mite uncomfort- able while Abby fussed about providing lunch for the lawman.

Birch waited until she had gone back into the kitchen, then asked quietly,

'Know your name. You pack a star at one time?'

'Long time ago,' Travis said, trying to sound casual but he knew there was tension in his tone just the same. 'Just casual work. Filled in as a deputy here and there, sheriff in a couple places.'

'One of them places wouldn't've been Wichita, would it? Say – couple years back?'

Travis looked at the man levelly. 'Maybe.'

Birch smiled faintly 'Yeah. Figured I knew the name ... you ain't been heard from since Wichita.'

There was a question in that remark and Travis deliberately ignored it.

'Like to ride far and wide,' was all he said, aware that the words sounded exactly what they were: an attempt to end the lawman's questions.

Lew Birch didn't seem inclined to curb his curiosity but as he opened his mouth to speak, Travis said quickly,

'I've heard of you, too. But not for some years. Often wondered what happened to you. You had quite a rep for bringing those trail towns to heel. They used to say you had to replace your gun-butts because you wore 'em out cuttin' notches in 'em...'

The steel-grey eyes drilled into the manager.

'I never notched my gun-butts. That was just talk. Matter of fact, I can remember every man I ever killed.'

Then he sighed. 'But them days are long gone. A man changes with the years.'

Cody Travis nodded slowly. 'Ain't that the truth,' he said quietly. 'You like a drink?'

'Sure – whiskey'd be fine.'

Travis went to the cupboard and poured the sheriff a stiff drink. As he handed it to the lawman, Birch asked mildly:

'You ain't drinkin'?'

'Not the hard stuff. Have a stomach problem and it aggravates it. Enjoy a beer though.'

'Uh-huh. Well, when you come to town, mebbe I'll buy you one.'

'Look forward to it.'

Birch raised his glass. 'Welcome to the Bitterroots. And good luck in your job.'

He tossed it down swiftly and then Abby came back carrying a tray of sandwiches and coffee, smiling.

'Let's eat, shall we? And you can tell us something about this wild country, Sheriff. And exactly what happened to Ross, the previous manager.'

Birch frowned. 'He drowned. Pure and simple.'

'Oh? I heard there was some doubt about the way he actually got into that river.'

'Now where did you hear a thing like that?'

Abby seemed tense now but forced a smile as she poured coffee.

'I think it was Mr Dysart mentioned it.'

But Travis, watching her closely, knew Dysart hadn't said anything of the sort. Not to him, anyway.

4

Bitterroot Country

'Christ! He's a drunk!'

Abe McKinley looked up from Stedmann's letter and laughed at Lew Birch and Stew Hagen as they stood in the shade of the tree down behind the forge.

'Cody Travis is a goddamn *drunk!* Stedmann says he was on the booze even in Wichita and then he shot down some trail boss and really took to the rotgut. They kicked him outta the sheriff's job there and no one heard of him for a couple years. Till now.'

'Hear tell Mrs Travis used to be a nurse. Mebbe she's been takin' care of him,' Birch opined.

'Hell, well that's good news anyways, Abe,' Hagen said. 'We don't have to worry none if he's a drunk.'

'Not sure he is,' said the sheriff and both men glanced at him sharply. 'Gave me a whiskey but didn't take any himself. Said it upset his stomach – says he only drinks beer. Sounds to me like he's been weaned off the booze and has to step lightly so he don't fall off the wagon.'

'Wonder if Dysart knows?' mused McKinley. 'Likely does – Travis is s'posed to be a friend of his. Well, we just gotta watch Mr T mighty close. A reformed drunk is like a man who's suddenly got religion. Wants everyone else to be the same as him an' won't bend the rules even a little.'

'I was you, I'd watch him close, for whatever reason,' Sheriff Birch said quietly. 'He might be a drunk or a reformed one now, but he was hell in a handbasket when he was totin' badge in some of them trail towns a few years back. Fists, guns, knife, anythin' at all. And he had no fear...'

'What turned him into a drunk then?' asked McKinley. 'You said he was on the booze before he went right off the rails after Wichita.'

'Heard it was a woman. Some said the trail boss he killed was mixed up in it somehow. I dunno the details. By the by, I delivered a letter to Mrs Travis, too. It had Dysart's name on the back.'

The ramrod frowned. 'Why's he writin' to her and not Travis?'

Birch shrugged, straightened his flat-crowned hat, tugging the narrower-than-usual brim down firmly. 'Just step easy for a spell, Abe. Have to get on back to town now.'

'Travis says Anders from Horseshoe's been bitchin' about his mavericks. Heard anythin'?'

Birch settled into the saddle and held the reins loosely as he looked down at the foreman. 'Sure. He came to me. I told him to complain to Dysart. Looks like he did.'

'Well, he better not do too much complainin'.'

'If he does, you leave things to me. We don't want any more men dyin' on this range.'

The sheriff turned his horse and rode away across the yard, around behind the bunkhouse, heading for the distant front gate.

'You think we really got anythin' to worry about with this Travis, Abe?' asked Stew Hagen. 'I mean, the woman seems to run him, an' now we learn he's a drunk...'

'Whether we got cause to worry or not, I'm *gonna* worry till we make sure just how the land lies,' answered Abe grimly. 'Dysart picked him for some reason. And I want to know what it is.'

Thistle's owner, Jock Dysart, had included a short note for Cody Travis with Abby's letter.

The manager read it swiftly; it merely confirmed his salary with the promise of a bonus if Travis improved the profits for the ranch. He showed it to Abby and she nodded and handed it back. Her own letter from Dysart was folded and she pushed it back into the envelope.

'Let's hope he has a big bonus in mind,' she said.

Travis frowned a little. He had been waiting for her to tell him what Dysart was writing to her about but she had made no effort to convey any information as yet. Now Cody gestured to the envelope she was placing in the pocket on the front of her dress.

'Dysart have anything interesting to say?'

She shook her head. 'Not really. He was just wishing us well in our married life and hoped I won't find it too lonely out here away from the company of other women.'

That was all she said and as she turned away, Travis spoke casually.

'Didn't mention anything more about

Ross's death being something other than an accident then?'

She turned quickly, her eyes flashing to his face, and then she smiled – a little stiffly.

'Why would he say anything like that?'

'You said he'd mentioned there was something funny about Ross's death.'

'Did I? Oh, well, he just said that Ross was an excellent horseman and he thought he would have been well aware that it was dangerous to ride on a cutbank at the edge of a fast-flowing river... What time do you leave on your ride?'

Changing the subject.

'Abe says we'll leave pretty soon. Sure you don't want to come? Looks like mighty fine country – rugged and wild, the way I like it.'

She wrinkled her nose – which action deepened his frown a little – and said, 'I like horse-riding, all right, but I don't think I want to go riding into wild canyons and those mountains just yet. I've plenty to do around here.'

'You gave me a lecture about our position. Why don't you get one of the Indian women to help you?'

'I probably will.' Abby regarded him soberly. 'You sound – put-out.'

'I just figured to come in smooth and easy,

feel my way. Didn't aim to get the crew's back up. Or McKinley's.'

She nodded gently, not moving her gaze from his face.

'Like I did, you mean. Perhaps I'm used to giving orders and running things – I *was* the matron of Dr Arnold's infirmary for several years. It's bound to have rubbed off.' She smiled as she put a hand on his arm and lifted to her toes to brush his cheek with her lips. 'But I'll watch in future that I don't upset your – sensibilities, Cody. The last thing I want to do is put you in a bad light. But I do want you to be a success and – I guess I tried too hard too soon.'

'OK.' He grinned, slid an arm about her waist and kissed her in return. 'See you around supper-time.'

She watched him walk out of the room, her teeth tugging lightly at her lower lip.

Yes – she would have to watch it, all right. She would have to tread very, very carefully!

'How come you don't wear a gun?' asked Abe McKinley as he led Travis between the hills and into the lower pastures where a lot of the cattle were grazing.

Travis slapped the butt of the rifle in the saddle boot. 'I've got this.'

64

'Sure, that's fine out here, but what about in town if you get into a fracas in a saloon or somewhere?'

'Don't go into saloons much any more. And there are other ways of settling trouble than with a sixgun.'

McKinley snorted. 'This is real wild country. Law ain't anythin' to write home about. Men sorta make their own even with Lew Birch packin' a star. You oughta play it safe.'

'When I think I need to wear a sixgun I likely will. There doesn't seem to be much graze.'

'No – lousy spring like I told you. Cows are eatin' low branches of trees fast as the new shoots appear. There'll be plenty of grass when it warms up.' He leaned from the saddle and pointed. 'See the snow still up there in the hollows?'

Travis looked and nodded. 'There'd be a lot of canyons in there.'

Abe straightened in the saddle, tried to sound casual. 'What makes you say that?'

'The look of the country. What I'm getting at is that most of the mavericks are still pretty young. If they haven't come down to lower pastures with their mothers, we'll have cows in there as well.'

'So?'

'I want them flushed out and brought down to the lower pastures. Longer you leave them with short graze, weaker they'll get and the more fat they'll lose...'

'Well, we've always left it to them to come on out when the weather warms...'

'Lazy way of doing it, and it could explain why Dysart's so disappointed with the profits. Get a bunch of men working in there first thing tomorrow. Camp out. Couple of riders can drive the day's round-up down to the bench and the flats by the creek.'

'Hell, they'll bitch about campin' out in the cold! Freeze your butt off here at night and it means takin' men off other jobs!'

'Then do it. Saving those cows is more important than anything else right now, and you'll be able to bring in the mavericks at the same time.'

It made good sense and Abe knew it. But he didn't want *all* the crew working that country.

And he sure didn't need Travis poking around in there, either.

'Hell almighty!'

The exclamation burst from him as Travis suddenly slid the Winchester from the saddle scabbard, threw it to his shoulder while

66

working the lever and fired the instant the butt was in position. Abe snapped his head up in the direction the smoking rifle was pointing and far up the slope he saw the brush surge and sway and then the body of a large whitetail deer crashed through and slid and tumbled down the slope.

'Judas priest!' exclaimed McKinley, somewhat shaken.

When they rode over, Abe saw the small patch of blood just behind the left leg. He turned slowly to look at Travis who hadn't dismounted and was holding the rifle with the butt resting on his leg.

'Man, I never even seen that whitetail!'

'Caught a glimpse of him through that chokecherry: the white patch gave him away.'

'But the angle...! You got him right through the heart! Must've dropped him where he stood!'

'Well, he had to step down to get past a rock and he showed enough of his quarter for me to get a bead.'

McKinley was more than impressed. A man with eyesight like that – *and the lightning reactions* – well, he would be a man to be reckoned with.

'I'll have Kiley come out and bring in the

carcass, for the cook to skin and butcher.' He forced a grin. 'Couple of days on venison steaks won't get you much gripin' from the boys.'

'You seem to like doing things the easy way Abe. We'll hang that deer from a tree and then slash it so it'll be bled by the time Kiley comes for it.'

McKinley pursed his lips, and they locked gazes for a long minute. Then Abe lifted the deer effortlessly across his shoulders, walked across to a tree and dumped it at the base. He took out his knife, cut the hind legs between the Achilles tendon and the bone, taking care not to cut the tendon. Then he broke off a branch while standing on his horse's back, lifted the carcass one-handed and pushed it on to the stub of the branch through the cuts he had made.

'Oughta keep any hungry mountain lion away till Kiley gets here. I can skin it out for the hide if you want…'

'Just cut its throat to let it bleed. Kiley can gut it when he gets here. You've made your point.'

'Sure,' Abe said dropping down to slash the stretched throat. 'See, it ain't so much a man bein' lazy as havin' his own way of doin' things.'

'Like I said, you've made your point. Now let's see what the trail's like for getting into the back country,' Travis said, sliding the Winchester back into the saddle scabbard. 'I want to see as much as I can of the range.'

'Sure thing.'

Travis smiled to himself as he saw the way Big Abe was regarding him now – there wasn't anything like respect there (McKinley would respect no man) but there was a wariness and maybe just a touch of apprehension.

Why there should be the latter he didn't know. But he aimed to find out.

Meantime, he would do all he could to encourage Abe's anxious feelings about him – at least until the man worked out that bringing down that whitetail simply *had* to be a lucky shot.

The deer carcass now hung from two S-shaped meat hooks in the cool-shed attached to the cookshack.

It was well ventilated as it had been built so as to catch the breeze that blew towards it. But Travis had plans to make it even better by adding moveable wooden baffles at the windows so that the breeze could be deflected into and through the building –

and on to its contents – no matter which direction it blew from.

Even the cook – called 'Hoppy' because of his one leg – liked the idea and gave it his grudging approval. But he was still mighty leery of Abby and had threatened to leave if she insisted on her stringent hygiene schedule.

'She's still a nurse at heart, Hoppy,' Travis told him. 'Damn good one, too. First time one of the men busts a leg or an arm or you cut yourself deep enough to hose the walls with your blood, you'll find out. Won't be any need to wait a day and a half for a doc to come out from town. She'll handle the wounds...'

It gave the cook something to think about, for most of the first aid fell to him and he was mighty rough and ready. In fact, two men had died because of his lack of medical knowledge. Might be something in staying on after all, he decided, if the woman would make things easier for him and, he supposed, it wasn't *too* much of a trial to wash his hands before handling the food or to scrub down the benches. Hell, he could even get one of the Injun women to do that chore.

Now, casually balanced on one of his

crutches, he cut strips of meat from the carcass that Kiley had skinned out, slapped them on to a rust-specked tray. He jumped, almost losing the crutch, when a voice behind him said,

'I hope you'll rinse off all that meat before you cook it and serve it up, Hoppy.'

It was the woman, of course, and he smothered a curse as he hacked savagely at some rump steaks, cutting them all raggedy. He slapped them on to the pile on the tray before turning to glare at Abby.

'I always wash the meat first, specially if I've dropped it in the dirt.'

'My God! You ought to throw those pieces out!'

Hoppy sighed. 'Ma'am, you are new to ranch livin'. There ain't no butcher's shop round the corner out here. We can't throw away grub an' waste it. Live here a spell and your stomach'll get used to things you never figured you could, would, or should, eat. But that's the way things is.'

'Then *things* may have to change,' she told him. 'But go ahead with your work – I like to see the way you slice the meat.'

'Remind you of when you was a nurse?'

Abby turned slowly at the sound of the deep voice and saw McKinley standing in the doorway, stooping because of the low ceiling. He came in, smiling crookedly.

'Once a nurse, always a nurse, they say huh?'

'Yes, I suppose so.' Abby spoke slowly, somehow uneasy with the man's bulk seeming to crowd the small shed. She jumped a little as she backed into the swaying carcass and McKinley reached out to steady her, his touch a lot more gentle than she would have expected.

He looked down into her face. 'Steady there...'

She pulled free, flushing a little, saw Hoppy looking from her to Abe before he returned to slicing the meat from the bones.

'That other thing they say about nurses true, too?' Abe asked.

'What other thing?' She sounded genuinely puzzled.

'You know – about workin' with all them men, washin' 'em all over, givin' the nurses a thrill and so on...'

'A sick person does not excite, Mr McKinley. They are to be regarded with sympathy and compassion and the only "thrill" a good nurse gets is when she has done her job well and set the patient on the road to recovery. *That* is one of the things they ought to say about nurses, but seldom do.'

McKinley grinned, leering a little. 'Well, I sure ain't heard it, but I've heard plenty about nurses knowin' how to keep a man happy ... an' willin' to do it.'

Hoppy coughed, feeling awkward, but the others paid him no attention. Abby looked coldly at the big foreman and said:

'You listen to too much gossip, Mr Mc-Kinley. I believe you'd do better to find ways to keep my husband happy. Your work here apparently leaves quite a lot to be desired. Now, get out of my way, please.'

Big Abe didn't like her speaking to him that way but he eased far enough back to let her by and then snarled at the cook to get on with his job.

'And I want three of the biggest steaks for my supper. And they'd better be cooked just the way I like 'em, savvy?'

Without waiting for an answer, he strode out, straightening a mite too soon and knocking off his hat going through the doorway. He picked the hat up angrily and slapped it against his trousers, raising small clouds of dust.

So Travis wasn't happy with his work, eh? Well, wasn't that just too blame bad!

Pretty soon now, there was going to be a

lot more Cody Travis wouldn't be happy about.

And that uppity wife of his!

Yeah, *real* soon...

It was time to test them both.

5

Testing Time

Kiley was the one selected to put Travis to the test.

'Aw, shoot, Abe,' griped the flat-faced man. 'How about Wrango? He's meaner an' tougher'n me.'

'I might need Wrango for somethin' else. Now you do like I say. If he fires you, head up for the maverick canyon and lay low. I want you for anythin' I'll send word, likely by Stew. But you don't make a move till I say, savvy?'

Kiley nodded, surly. 'I hope there's a bonus in this.'

'There will be – one way or another.'

Kiley didn't know what that meant but McKinley didn't offer any explanation, merely turned on his heel and strode away across the yard.

Cody Travis had no idea he was walking into anything when he saw Kiley piddling about around the barn. The ranch manager stepped out of the office on to the porch.

'Thought you were s'posed to be on round-up on the south range?' he called. Kiley didn't look up from whatever he was doing – looked like he was whittling a stick. Cody raised his voice. 'Kiley, I'm talking to you!'

'Yeah?' Kiley asked without looking up. 'What's up?'

'You're supposed to be on round-up.'

'Not today.'

It began to stir within him then: this was shaping up into deliberate provocation. Curious, Travis stepped down from the porch and started across the yard. He wasn't really surprised when he saw cowboys appearing from behind the barn, down by the forge, beyond corrals.

A waiting audience...

'Why not today, Kiley?' Travis asked quietly.

For the first time Kiley glanced up from the stick he was whittling; it had no particular shape, just a point hacked on and a pile of shavings at his feet and sticking to his dirty boots.

'Aw, got me a sore back.'

'You'd better let Mrs Travis take a look at it.'

Kiley shook his head. 'She ain't layin' a hand on me.'

'She's a good nurse.'

'A good *looker*, anyways. Dunno about the other.'

The gathered men laughed quietly and Travis was sure then: they'd set this up, likely to test him. He'd been going a mite easy – too easy, according to Abby – and now it was time for them to see how far they could push him.

O-K!

'Kiley – what you've got is a sore head, not a sore back. And not enough brains to know the difference.'

There was silence from the onlookers and Kiley squinted, his clasp-knife half-way through shaving more wood from the stick. He narrowed his small eyes and curled a lip, a mite surprised that Travis was carrying this to him now.

'I know the difference between a man and a feller who runs around hangin' on to a woman's skirts.'

That brought a laugh. But not from Travis.

'Prove it to me.'

'Huh!'

'Oh, for Chrissake,' sighed Travis stepping forward. 'Let's get this over with, there's

77

work to be done.'

His hand darted out, grabbed the wrist of the hand holding the knife, twisted violently so that Kiley yelled and came up on to his toes as his arm was wrenched behind his back. His nerveless fingers dropped the knife, but he recovered and stabbed at Travis's face with the sharpened stick. Cody dodged but the wood caught the skin of his neck, drew blood, then snagged in his jacket.

He butted Kiley in the face and the man's nose went with an audible crack. He howled and clapped both hands to his face, blood oozing between his fingers. Travis belted him two solid blows in the midriff. Kiley staggered, reeling. Travis went after him almost lazily, grabbing his shoulder, spinning him around to face him, and then hooking two more savage blows into the midriff. The impact lifted Kiley's feet off the ground. He faltered and Travis grabbed him by an ear and clubbed a blow into the pain-twisted flat face. His fist skidded off the blood and Kiley made a feeble attempt to go on the offensive. But he was hurt – badly.

Travis set his boots squarely, hammered a barrage on the man's lower ribs and when he sagged, hit him on the side of the neck.

Kiley dropped to his knees, gasping. Travis kicked him in the chest and stretched him out.

He planted a boot on Kiley's neck, leaning down, breathing a little hard.

'You've been used, Kiley, and you're a fool for letting it happen. Draw your time. You're finished on Thistle.'

The men were silent and Travis raked them with his cold eyes. 'You men get back to work – and I mean now.'

No one gave him an argument.

He washed face and hands under the pump that McKinley had fixed and straightened slowly, water dripping from his hard features as a big shadow fell across him. It was McKinley and, beyond the wide shoulders, he saw the cowboys gathering saddles and tools and choosing work horses, ready to go about their chores. Kiley was crawling towards the bunkhouse, coughing rackingly.

'No man'd do that to me,' Big Abe said flatly.

'Nor me,' Travis answered, using a kerchief to wipe his face, then he wrapped the damp cloth around his throbbing knuckles. 'Satisfied now?'

McKinley arched his eyebrows then frowned. 'Dunno what you're gettin' at. But you seem to be tougher than you look.'

'Just like my orders to be obeyed. Which reminds me, aren't you supposed to be organizing the men into round-up and branding teams?'

'I'll get around to it.'

'Get around to it now,' Travis told him, eyes flinty and unwavering. 'You've seen how far I'll push before I push back.'

'Mebbe,' McKinley said with a look of arrogance. 'Or mebbe you were just lucky, struck Kiley on a bad day.'

'Well, he's having a bad day now. Anyone else wants to buck me can join him.'

McKinley looked surprised, seeing that Travis was serious. He scoffed. 'You can't fire 'em all!'

'Why? Plenty of men looking for work in the spring, pockets and bellies empty after a hard winter. I could replace the lot of you overnight.'

Abe's eyes narrowed. 'You includin' me?'

Travis merely continued to stare.

'Heeeyyy – you *are* an arrogant sonuver, ain't you?' Abe leaned slightly forward. 'But I don't leave anywhere till I'm good and ready.'

'We'll sort things out when the time comes, Abe. Meanwhile, get those men organized.'

Travis walked back towards the house. McKinley stood watching him climb the porch steps and then enter the office by the side door.

'That son of a bitch has somethin' special comin'!' he muttered, then wheeled and began bawling out men's names, bringing them running across the yard.

They all recognized that tone in Big Abe's voice: it said plainly, *Don't mess with me this day!*

'You let them get to you,' Abby said, taking his hand out of the bowl of warm water he was soaking it in and pressing a cold cloth across his throbbing knuckles.

'Just figured it was time to let 'em get their test over with. Knew it had to come.'

'Why Kiley? I thought it might be McKinley who forced a showdown.'

Travis shook his head. 'He's saving himself for something bigger. There's something going on that some of the crew are in on. I've been trying to figure out who's in and who isn't. So far I reckon Stew Hagen, Kiley, Wrango and maybe Race Satterfield. Might be another one or two I'm not sure about yet.'

She glanced at him sharply. 'What do you

think it is?'

'Likely something to do with the mavericks. Abe got a little fussed when I braced him about it and told him Anders from Horseshoe had complained to Dysart.'

'What, exactly?' She was interested although she appeared to be concentrating on his hand.

It was a way she had: she showed interest in his work – whether it was feigned or genuine sometimes he wasn't sure but it gave him a good feeling.

'Well, a maverick has no brand till a man burns one on it. Could be that Abe and his bunch are making themselves a little money on the side. Been known to happen plenty of times.'

She frowned. 'They brand mavericks, gathered from wherever they find them and – then what?'

'Run 'em out at night to someone who'll buy, no questions asked.'

'Surely that's rustling!'

'That's what it is.'

'But – where could they do it? I mean, I know little about ranching, but where could they hide the mavericks while they brand them and, presumably, fatten them a little, before driving them out?'

'Thistle is a big place. Those hills are riddled with hidden canyons. They could do it, all right.'

Her teeth tugged at her lower lip. 'How will you find out for sure?'

'Locate the place they're hiding them, hole up and wait and catch them redhanded.'

She sucked in a sharp breath. 'That's – dangerous!'

'Dysart's paying me to run this spread at a profit. If I let half the crew steal him blind, I'm not doing my job.'

She smiled faintly, leaned down and planted a kiss lightly on his forehead.

'Mr Dysart sure is lucky he hired a man like you. Perhaps I could help. They'll be watching you, specially now you've shown them you won't be pushed around. I could go for rides and I wouldn't be suspect. If you tell me what to look for...'

'No. This is my chore.'

'But I'm sure I could do it.'

'So am I – but you ain't doing it. You said you're not all that keen on riding but go if you want. Just take in the scenery. Don't try to search out their maverick canyon or you'll find out that the legend about Western men always respecting women just ain't true. Not all of the time.'

He thought she lost a little colour and he felt her tremble as she lifted his hand and placed it back into the bowl of warm water to help reduce the swelling.

'I *want* to help, Cody.' She spoke quietly but the intensity of her words brought a frown to his face. 'If these men are doing what you think, they've got to be stopped.' Then her eyes flashed and he was puzzled to see they were moist, her mouth tight as she asked, 'Would they – kill, if someone caught them at this rustling?'

'They might. Likely would.'

'Then don't you think it's time you started wearing your sixgun, again?'

He squirmed a little, removed his hand from the bowl and picked up a cloth to dry it. He didn't look at her as he said,

'Not yet. I'll – leave it a little longer.'

Her lips compressed but she didn't try to argue with him.

The weather turned bad for a few days with sleet and bitter cold and the cowboys spent miserable hours in the saddle. Cattle and calves bawled pitifully. Horses huddled in bunches in the corrals. The short grass cracked underfoot with frost, and the fireplaces in the ranch house and bunkhouse burned night and day.

Then, as it often did in this country, it suddenly brightened into the bluest thing God ever made – a wide Montana sky, totally free of cloud, the sun warming the air enough for men to shed heavy jackets and work in woollen shirts.

Abe McKinley, of course, walked around the sunny yard stripped to the waist, showing his muscled torso, carrying out his anvil exercises. Abby watched from the bedroom window and said once, while Travis was dressing;

'He certainly is a Greek god walking.'

Cody smiled crookedly. 'Want me to pass along that observation to him?'

She spun quickly. 'Don't you dare!'

'Might be persuaded not to – whoa! Not right now. Have to go check on the herds.'

'How romantic! But I'd like to ride along, Cody. I haven't seen much of this place yet and, after all, it is going to be home for – well, quite some time.'

He saw no reason why she shouldn't come, and McKinley, still stripped to the waist and carrying a small tree that had been felled to make way for an extension to the barn on one shoulder, watched them ride out.

Stew Hagen was getting ready to ride to the southwest range and McKinley called him across, dumping the tree with a thud, brushing bark from his shoulder.

'You get a chance, check the maverick canyon. Tell Kiley I'll have a job for him so to stand by. Wrango said there were a couple cows dead in the south-west. Looked like they'd been chewed on by a grizzly.'

'More likely the cold killed 'em and a griz found 'em–'

'Sure, but it'd be somethin' a good manager'd want to check on. Just make sure you ain't followed.'

By mid-morning, they had ridden half-way round the pastures the men were working and Abby was fascinated to see some big-horn sheep high up on the steep slopes, bounding from rock to rock with an agility she thought bordered on the impossible.

'Most agile animal in the world, they say,' Travis said, dismounting behind a rock and getting out the field-glasses. 'And with the sharpest eye.'

He focused on a group on the peak and handed the glasses to Abby. She watched, sweeping the countryside, while he rolled and lit a cigarette.

'There's a lone one! He seems to be cling-ing to the side of an almost vertical cliff!'

Travis took the glasses, found the sheep, and Abby made to stand up from behind the rock where they were sheltering from a cool wind knifing down from the ridge.

'Don't move! You'll spook him.'

She looked at him, astonished. 'From here? Why that peak must be – two or three miles away. He doesn't show very large in the glasses.'

He handed her the field glasses. 'Keep focused on him.'

She found the sheep again and then Travis stood and walked out from behind the rock. Within seconds the sheep's head swung up and he turned on his precarious perch to face in their direction, neck arched, his whole body in an alert position.

'I don't believe it!' Abby gasped. 'He saw you!'

'Keep watching.' Travis turned and walked to a slope and dropped down it. The moment he dropped below the top, the sheep bounded away, seeming almost to fly across the acute slope, leaping without hesitation from one tiny foothold to the next, angling up even higher, finally dis-appearing behind the rocks.

Travis smiled at the expression on Abby's face. 'He'll run for five or six miles before he stops to graze again. Hardest animal ever to stalk and shoot.'

'I can barely believe what I've seen,' she said, still sweeping the countryside, looking for more bighorns. She paused, refocused and said sharply, 'Cody! There's a rider coming out from between those two hills... It looks like Stew Hagen.'

Travis frowned, took the glasses. 'Now what in hell's he doing up there? He's miles away from the regular pastures...'

'You said you thought he might be one of the maverick rustlers...'

He nodded, absently grinding out his cigarette underfoot now. 'I'll need to take a look in there.'

'Now?'

'No – I'll ride back to the ranch with you. Now don't get that look, Abby. You're not going in there. If I jump 'em there might be shooting. At the very least it's typical grizzly country ... c'mon. Let's start riding back. And keep this hill between us and Hagen. I don't want him to know we've been in the vicinity.'

'Cody – I think you should teach me how to shoot.'

Travis waited on the hogback just a little north of the spread while Abby reluctantly rode on down to the ranchyard. Big Abe McKinley came out from behind the barn, carrying an armload of newly planed planks for the extension.

He grinned at Abby as she dismounted by the corrals, admiring her figure in the corduroy trousers.

'Your man comin' down?'

Abby glanced up to where Travis was still sitting his mount on the hogback.

'No – he was just seeing me home. He's going back into the hills.'

Abe cupped his hands around his mouth as Travis started to turn away.

'Bud Corey just rode in, said Stew Hagen told him there's two or three dead cows in the south-west pasture. Looked like a grizzly had nailed 'em.'

Travis hesitated, then waved acknowledgement.

'I'll check it out.' As he heeled his mount forward, he wondered how Hagen had been able to give Corey that message when he and Abby had seen the man miles to the north.

Abe, his torso gleaming with sweat, walked over to Abby. He brushed against her deliberately as he edged her gently aside.

'I'll unsaddle for you, ma'am. Be my pleasure to take care of you while your man's away.'

'Thanks, anyway, Abe. But I can take care of myself.'

'Sure. But the offer stands. Any time you want me to help out, any way I can – why just you holler. Any time at all.'

Abby frowned as she made her way back towards the house. The words were simple enough, polite, even, but somehow they unsettled her.

6

Bear Trap

It was less than pleasant cutting open the stomachs of the dead cows.

It was cold in the mostly unused pasture and there were four carcasses now, one more than Big Abe had reported. Two of the animals that had obviously died early had been already mostly eaten by a bear – he found only one set of tracks, and they were *big*, with long claws on front and back pawprints. The cows' stomachs were gone. But the third one, which had had some meat torn out, still had its stomachs. The fourth cow had not yet been attacked by the bear; it had apparently died too recently for that.

Travis started on this animal; it was obvious that it had died of something other than bear attack and while it had been cold, he didn't think the temperature would have been low enough to kill the cow. His hands were numb and he used his blade carefully.

In the cow's second stomach he found

what he was looking for: small hard balls that looked like berries and some fresh leaf-shoots, partly masticated and digested.

'Frosted oak,' he said aloud and with a certain satisfaction. He had seen it before and though it wasn't fully understood as yet, he knew it had something to do with the early buds after a bitter winter producing a special kind of sap that protected against freezing, and it was mighty toxic to cattle. But hungry cows weren't able to resist the fresh leaf-growth and buds when grass was so short. They filled their bellies, only to die not long after. Travis was just thankful that most of the cows that would normally use this pasture had been driven down to lower grass which was beginning to thrive. Only a few wanderers remained up here and most of them had likely been scared off by the bear.

He was putting the 'frosted oak' in his saddle-bags when he smelled something – something primal, reeking of the woods and the wild, the gamey, driedsweat, musty and unwashed odour of an animal not long out of hibernation.

Skin prickling and the short hairs on the back of his neck beginning to stand up, Cody Travis turned quickly – and there he was. A huge bear skulking just at the edge of the timber and brush, on all fours, watching him, a little drool hanging from the lower jaw in a swaying silver thread.

At the same time, the horse sensed the animal and, with a whinny, lurched away, knocking Travis sprawling. He rolled and instinctively shouted for the animal to come back. His rifle was still in the saddle scabbard and he was not wearing a sixgun.

By then the bear had reared up with a snarling cough and smashed through the remaining screen of brush, mad as hell, and dropping back to all fours as it lunged towards him. Travis was already bouncing to his feet and running, noted the animal favoured its right foreleg, but it wasn't slowing him down any. He started to chase the horse but knew it was useless. He would never catch it and its terror would keep it running far and long. He really didn't want to see how close the bear was but knew he had to look. He glanced over his shoulder, breath hissing.

Too blame close! His mind screamed when he saw it coming, unstoppable, claws tearing loose great clods of grass and soil, the drool streaming back over its dished face. That feature and the colour of the coat, with the slight silver sheen on the ends of the hairs, together with the tracks he had found with the two-inch claws, made it a grizzly for sure and not the less aggressive black bear that occasionally roamed this far west. Probably, it looked upon him more as a trespasser on its territory than as a meal, and would be satisfied just to chase him out of the area. *He hoped!* Still, he would be a dead man if the bear got within striking distance.

For a moment he wasted breath cursing the horse, then put in an extra effort as he felt the ground rise beneath his feet. He tripped, half-sprawled, but instead of thrusting upright again – the slope was abruptly steeper now – he clawed at the ground and thrust with his legs, going up without losing much speed. He heard the bear's deep grunts of frustration and anger as it came bounding after him, still with that lopsided gait. Travis felt a tightening band clamping around his chest, breath rasping his throat, a pressure of pounding blood behind his eyes and in his ears.

Then something touched his left heel, rough and hard, swiping one leg so violently across the other that for a moment he thought it was going to pop clear out of his hip-socket. He lashed out with a kick, catching the bear in one eye, throwing it off balance. It scrambled in an effort to keep from falling. Travis started to slide back and he knew this was the end that every man feared – being eaten alive by a wild animal. His knife would be less than useless but it was all he had. He snatched at the hilt just as his body struck a rock which stopped his fall.

The bear had been too confident, certain that the swipe that had connected with Cody's boot – incidentally ripping loose the high heel – would bring the man tumbling down the slope into his waiting jaws. So the grizzly had stopped and reared on to its hind legs, a terrifying nine feet high, Travis judged, but he only thought about the height much later. Then Travis's body hung up on the rock and the bear was still standing, waiting. Cody got his boots against the rock and thrust wildly, clawing with his hands, breaking horny fingernails in his efforts as he literally hurled himself upslope, away from the animal. He was just below the crest, panting, slipping, legs going frantically He flung his chest on to the ridgetop, dug in his boot-toes and kicked himself across, starting to slide and skid and roll down the far side. He heard the bear's roar and then the snarling and the sounds of the slope being torn up as the grizzly lunged towards the top.

When it appeared, Travis barely glimpsed it as he spun and rolled and skidded down. He managed to get control of the slide and swung his legs downslope. Below him on a small flat outcrop, stood his horse, panting, sweating, blowing, calmer now that the bear wasn't in sight. The horse was looking back across the face of the slope, concentrating, searching for the bear, but in the wrong direction.

Then it heard Travis sliding down. The grey looked up sharply, glimpsed the bear bounding over the ridge on all fours. The horse whinnied and gathered itself to lunge away. Desperately, Travis hurled himself bodily at the big grey, diving off the slope. He caught a stirrup and was dragged off his feet as the mount thrust away in terror. He pulled himself half-upright but couldn't get his legs under him or reach the saddle. So he flung himself in a wild lunge for the scabbard, hands clawed, wrapping around the smooth leather, fingers almost tearing loose from their joints as he dug in his broken nails and let his full weight drop on to the leather sheath.

He hung suspended for a few moments and then the rawhide thonging that held the scabbard to the saddle snapped and he fell, kicking away quickly from the grey's flying hoofs. He clutched the scabbard to his chest as he rolled on to the narrow ledge, to free the rifle. The grizzly, only five yards away, reared up on to its hind legs, snarling, spittle flying as it shook its head, ugly teeth bared, coming for him. Travis fired through the end of the scabbard, missing the bear, but finally flinging the scabbard aside.

Supported on one knee he worked lever and trigger and put three fast shots into the hairy body. The bear wrenched right and left with the strike of bullets, blood splashed the fur, but it kept lumbering forward. Frantic now, Travis shot again, into the centre of the chest. The beast stopped dead, then shook itself and came charging on.

Cody Travis groaned, knowing he only had two shots left. He aimed for an eye and fired from a distance of less than two yards. The bear screamed and threw back its head, blood streaming, jaws agape, red and raw and wet-looking as it came for him.

In desperation, Travis rammed the rifle barrel into those gaping jaws, nauseated by the blast of hot, fetid breath, felt the rifle muzzle jar against the back of the throat. Then, as the bear slapped at the gun, he angled it up and fired, blasting the savage brain to jelly.

The bear fell towards him, its bulk catching his shoulder and sending him sprawling. Travis felt something across one leg, kicked wildly and just managed to get the limb out from under as 500 pounds of now-dead power and savagery collapsed. One flailing arm slashed him across the chest, tore his jacket and shirt. He felt the claws rake his flesh, dragging parallel bloody gashes.

Then the body slipped away from him and struck the edge of the ledge, tumbled over and continued on down the steep slope to bring up against the base of a sour oak with a thud that made the whole ridge tremble...

Travis lay there, incredulous that he was still alive and had lost no more than a few inches of flesh, one shirt and jacket, and the heel of a boot.

He stood up, legs trembling, his rifle empty and with no more ammunition for it – the jacket pocket that had been torn off by the bear had contained ten cartridges, but they were lost now, scattered somewhere downslope.

He sat there with his head resting on his arms across his drawn-up knees, letting his heart settle. He had no idea how much time passed, but he glimpsed the big grey, far over on the next ridge, just standing, looking for the bear, still badly spooked. He tried to whistle it up but his mouth was far too dry.

Then as he stood and made to climb down towards the dead bear – there was something he wanted to check about that animal – he heard a second horse, to his left, in the timber.

He spun that way, shading his eyes, glimpsed a rider weaving between the trees, heading across the slope slightly above him, parallel with the ridge.

He blinked a few times and wiped his eyes which were still hazy from his efforts. The rider was going away from him, leaning forward over his mount's neck – it looked like a strawberry roan.

Very much resembling the private mount that Kiley had used on the ranch.

No one had asked her to, but Abby Travis decided to go over the ranch books and ledgers. Travis had been checking through some when he had time, but mostly he was involved with the day-to-day running of the ranch. When you got right down to it, Cody simply didn't like bookwork.

She knew he had the intelligence to understand the records but he was short on patience with this kind of thing, preferred to be out and doing. This was a common enough symptom of a man reformed not all that long ago from alcoholism; it was one way of covering a lack of self-confidence.

In the clinic, she had been the one to nurse him through to his recovery and she had found Travis much more interesting than the average patient. Over a period of time he had told her about Bill Rankin, starting when they were naïve runaways, later sidekicks, setting out to conquer the world and the Wild West in particular.

Like young men everywhere with the sap singing in their veins they had been reckless, lived like there was no tomorrow, drank heavily as a means of releasing the tensions and boredom associated with cattle drives and ranching and plain drifting through the West. They believed like thousands before them that hard drinking was necessary for acceptance by the rough, tough men they rode with.

Travis, being more sensitive than Rankin,

had found himself beginning to depend more and more on alcohol and soon came to look upon it as a means of helping him forget most of his problems. For a time, at least. Bill, easier-going and none too observant, had been glad to pour the booze into his pard whenever he figured he needed to take on a load. Just as long as they had fun, what the hell?

Then, almost inevitably, they had fallen out over a girl. Holly – he had never told Abby Holly's second name, not that it mattered. She was not a professional whore, inasmuch as she did not operate from one of the hundreds of cat-houses in the cowtowns frequented by Rankin and Travis. But she would give her favours to any man she liked well enough and if he wanted to leave her a few dollars or a gift in appreciation, why, Holly saw no harm in taking it. She seemed to like Travis the best and this galled Rankin at times, especially when she refused to go with him because she preferred Cody's company.

Travis developed a fixation about her, decided she was the only woman who could really help him relax – she was a good listener and good-hearted, and genuinely felt sorry for the mixed-up cowboy. (He seemed to have some guilt about having run off from a brutal father – thereby leaving his long-suffering mother and sisters without even his meagre protection.) Bill, insensitive to Travis's developing obsession with Holly, moved in whenever he could, and there came a time when he forced himself upon her, giving her his hard mouth first, and, finally, his hard fists.

Cody, drunk, had fought with Bill and it had been a vicious, knock-down, drag-out brawl, both men needing medical attention afterwards. The sheriff of the town where it happened refused to let them ride out unless there was a three-day gap between each man's quitting the town: time enough to cool off, he reckoned. First man had to ride to the next town and send a telegraph message to the lawman that said he had arrived, the message also to be signed by the local sheriff. Only then would he let the second man go.

He meant well and it worked in one way: Rankin and Travis went their own trails and didn't meet again for long hard years. Then in the streets of Wichita, with Bill deliberately defying Travis, who was then sheriff, it had come to a shoot-out and Travis had killed Bill. Afterwards he hit the booze and went downhill rapidly until someone had brought him to Doctor Arnold's clinic and the good medico had kept him there, trying out his personal methods of curing a man of alcoholism...

It worked and during that time Travis had spoken of his life to Abby on many an occasion. He didn't know what had happened to Holly but that didn't seem to matter now. What bothered Travis most was this: he had been a little drunk when Bill Rankin had called him out in the streets of Wichita, and this may have accounted for the fact that his bullet had been lethal when he had meant only to wound his former pal.

But the thing he couldn't get out of his mind was that he had been thinking about Holly while Rankin had been raising hell in the saloons with his crew and then had come the square-off. Did he *deliberately* provoke the gunfight, or at least let it reach the point of no return – *then shoot to kill...?*

That was what had driven him to drink and set him on the long slide downhill until he had ended up in Abby's care at the clinic...

And somehow she had fallen for him and become Mrs Cody Travis.

Now she wanted to help him make this job a success: she owed him *that* much, she figured.

She had kept records and the accounts for Doctor Arnold, so knew a little of the basics of book-keeping. She was only vaguely familiar with the way tally figures worked but thought she understood it quite well enough to make at least some sense out of it all.

Still she wasn't good enough to decide whether the figures were exactly as they seemed, high at time of round-up (in a rough field-count) but disproportionately short when it came to branding and herd-ing-to-market time. There could be many reasons for the difference, she supposed, but decided she would have to ask Cody, or, perhaps Big Abe McKinley. But she decided against this latter almost immediately.

Then she found a well-worn ledger used for the wages and only minutes after flipping back through the pages, she saw something she didn't like – didn't like *at all!*

She studied it for a spell, checked to make sure the situation was as it seemed, then went out on to the porch. Big Abe Mc-Kinley was working down by the cattle-dip trough, repairing the tank which had been leaking badly; some calves, not knowing any better, had licked up the spilled milky fluid and had become so sick they had to be destroyed.

Abby was amazed to find herself just a little short of breath as she watched Abe's torso rippling with his movements, oily with sweat. Then, angry with herself, she cleared her throat and called:

'Abe! Abe, can you come up here – right away?'

McKinley waved acknowledgement, wiped his chest and arms with a rag and winked at the two men who had been helping him.

'You hear that? *Right away*, she says. Like all my women, just can't wait to get her hands on me!'

He walked unhurriedly towards the house and the two cowpokes glanced at each other, looking mildly worried, yet half-amused at the same time.

'Someone's in for a surprise,' opined a man called Southpaw.

'Yeah – wonder which one?' said the second man.

When Abby saw the big man coming across the yard, she turned back into the ranch office, leaving the door open.

7

Return

It was just on dark when Travis rode into the Thistle ranch yard.

He was forking a dun gelding that he had picked up at the river pasture round-up camp. Bud Corey was bossing that outfit and had sent a man to look for Travis's still-spooked grey, somewhere up in the hills yet, no doubt watching for bears around every corner.

Some of the men who had been working closer to the ranch were in the yard now, all ready for supper. They looked kind of guilty and caught-out when Travis dismounted stiffly by the corrals.

'You early birds had better have left nighthawks to watch the herd,' he said and there was a shuffling amongst the men. Finally two of them hurriedly saddled horses and rode out. Travis shook his head in disgust, but was puzzled by the small bunch of men he knew had been doing chores around the ranch and the way they were watching him now. Expectantly. *Something was up.*

It might have been his shredded jacket and the torn shirt or the grimy rags Corey's crew had used to bandage the slashes on his chest, but they seemed to have a leeriness about them as they watched his every movement. He took his rifle and examined it: the bear, when he had tried to slap it away from his mouth, had actually bent the barrel and there were two broken teeth caught in the wooden fore-end. Beyond being a souvenir of a frightening incident, the weapon wasn't much good for anything else.

He glanced towards the house as the door opened and he stiffened as Big Abe McKinley came out on to the porch, looking a little wild and dishevelled. Abe stopped dead when he saw Travis, pursed his lips, then started down the steps with that arrogant swagger. At the bottom he set his boots wide, hands on his hips, smiling crookedly. *Kind of – challenging – or maybe the only way out of – something...*

'Damn! You still walkin' around?' The giant shook his head in disbelief. 'You sure are full of surprises. Well, I got one for you but don't you go gettin' all fussed, now. She invited me in.' He gestured in the general direction of the yard crew. 'Ask Southpaw or Race – they heard her.'

Frowning, Travis naturally looked towards the two men and he felt his guts knot up as they nodded, backing up the ramrod.

'The hell've you done to her?' Travis asked Abe quietly and the big man's shoulders shrugged, a lip curled.

'Nothin' she didn't want me to... Thing is, *boss*, what you aim to do to *me*? You gonna fire me? Spank me, maybe...'

That one got a laugh from the gathering cowboys and Abe played to his audience, grinning at them, at the same time making sure he had all of Travis's attention.

'Din' I tell you she could hardly wait to get her hands on me, boys...? Little later, I'll give you the details – *all* the details.'

Travis was standing squarely in front of McKinley. He knew the man was spoiling for a fight, wanted to break him in two in front of these men. He had been holding it in for a long time. Now, it seemed he had decided it was right for a showdown... *Something had spurred him into making his move.*

So, without warning or any change of

expression, Cody Travis kicked him between the legs.

It was a savage, brutal kick with all of Travis's weight behind it and the sodden thud it made could be heard clear down to the barn.

Abe McKinley didn't fold up or stagger back. He simply collapsed, his legs going out from under him as if yanked by a rope attached to a bucking Missouri mule. His face rapped the gravel and there was a strange animal sound coming out of his lips with balls of spittle: something like a mixture of a man blowing across the mouth of an empty whiskey jug and the strangled, high-pitched scream of a jackrabbit as the coyote's jaws snapped closed on its throat.

Travis knew even then that it was a sound these men would remember for a long time. And he *wanted* them to remember this night for as long as they worked for Thistle.

He turned to the corral and took down a coiled lariat, stiff with dirt and animal sweat from use on round-up. He stood over the slowly writhing, retching McKinley.

'Plenty of women have fallen for that Greek-god face of yours, Abe, but they ain't gonna look on you with bedroom eyes for quite some time from now on.'

He flung the man on to his back and Abe groaned and pulled his knees up, still more or less paralysed and in extreme pain. Travis smashed him across the contorted face with the lariat coils. Dust and grit flew from the lay of the grass-plaited rope. Abe's head snapped to one side as the rough coils ripped his face raw.

The rope slashed back and forth relentlessly and Abe's features were hidden by a mask of blood and torn, swollen flesh. Breathing heavily, Travis saw a movement out of the corner of his eye on the porch but didn't look that way: *If she'd come out to watch, then she hadn't seen anything yet!*

He tossed the blood-stained rope aside, straddled the barely conscious McKinley and dragged and heaved the man to the corral fence. Gasping with the effort, he lifted Abe's upper body and propped the man's chest on the bottom bar. Then he picked up the lariat again, uncoiled a few feet, doubled it, and lashed the man's perfect, muscular back a dozen times. It didn't look so perfect by the time he had finished, the once-smooth flesh lacerated with cross-cross slashes and welts.

'Cody! For God's sake!'

He glanced towards the porch as he

blotted sweat from his forehead – and stiffened. She was there all right, leaning on the rail. But not casually – she was using the rail for support.

Her clothing was torn, her hair dishevelled. He could see that one side of her face was swollen and there was dried blood around her mouth.

Shaking, he walked across.

'He said you – invited him in. Two of the men backed him up...'

She stared at him out of a face that was more battered close-up than he had thought. Her lower lip was split and her words were slurred when she said, 'I – did – I found something in the – wages book I wanted him to – explain. He – began pawing me and...'

'Where'd you put my sixgun?' he gritted starting up the steps but she blocked his path.

'Don't, Cody – it'd be cold-blooded murder if you killed him now. You've – destroyed him. Leave it at that. Please.'

Her moist eyes searched his grim face: she was shocked by what she saw there, a merciless savagery she hadn't known was within him, although some of the stories she had heard about him of when he was a lawman in top form had shaken her. But, of course, she hadn't believed them. Now she saw how they could be true.

After all this time, Cody Travis had returned to the tough, relentless badge-toter he had been before the booze had almost destroyed him.

What was worse, she realised now that she had lost control. He was a man in charge of himself again and somehow it frightened her a little.

He swung away across the darkening yard, raking his bleak eyes around the silent men who were staring at the bloody, groaning figure of Abe McKinley. Travis scooped a pail of water from the horse-trough, threw it over Abe. The man started to come round and Travis tipped a second pail over him. Then he slapped the man back and forth across the torn face.

'You hear me, Abe? Get off Thistle within the next hour or I'll kill you. Take your men with you. Stew Hagen, Wrango, Satterfield, Southpaw, you know the ones I mean. I see any of you within a frog's leap of Thistle's line and I'll shoot you on sight. You think I'm bluffing, you still be here one minute past the deadline...'

Then he kicked Abe under the jaw and turned to the men. 'You know who I mean.

Pack your gear and get. You can pick up any wages owing at Lew Birch's office in town. Now *move!*'

The men scattered and Travis walked up on to the porch and slipped an arm about Abby's waist.

'Let's get you fixed up.'

She hesitated. 'Perhaps I'd better – see to McKinley. You gave him a terrible working-over.'

'He's alive. The others'll rope him to his bronc if they have to. Forget Big Abe. I've a notion he ain't gonna seem *quite* so big from here on in.'

He had the Indian women bring pails of hot water and fill the zinc hip-bath. He helped Abby undress, lips tightening when he saw the body bruises. She stood and let him look, then reached out a hand that shook a little and touched his stubbled face.

'I like the way you look at me, Cody. And, just for the record, no, he didn't manage full ... rape.' She almost smiled. 'When you've been nursing as long as I have, you learn a few tricks that most times prevent success...'

'You've got plenty of guts, Abby. I'll leave you to soak a while. You just call if you want anything.'

'Before you go – what happened to your chest?'

'Bear scratched me. Leave it for now.'

He left quietly and she was grateful for his thoughtfulness in giving her this time alone, soaking away the aches and pains from Abe McKinley's blows and savage gropings. It was brutal what Travis had done to the man, but she had no sympathy for McKinley. Maybe she should have let Travis finish the job.

Then she eased her battered body into the soothing warm water with the soap suds spilling over the side of the small bath.

Travis was in the parlour with coffee on a tray, waiting. He poured her a cup and she sipped gratefully.

'A bear?' she asked, sitting on the arm of his chair. She smelled of soap and talcum and he smiled as he placed a hand on her thigh and told her about the bear attack.

'My God! You were very lucky!'

'Yeah. I thought the bear was favouring one leg and I took a look after he was dead. He'd been wounded – and not long before I showed in that pasture. It was a bullet wound. Got him good and mad at us humans before I arrived and started working on those dead cows, which by that time he'd marked out for himself in his territory. If he hadn't been hurt he might've been content just to chase me off, but by then he was wanting to kill the first man he saw.'

'Are you saying ... someone deliberately wounded him before you arrived? To get him good and mad?'

He nodded. 'That's the way I figure it. Abe told me about the dead cows as you know. Said Bud reported 'em to Stew Hagen. But after I'd killed the bear I was afoot and I walked down to the river camp. Bud Corey said he hadn't been back to the ranch, hadn't seen either Abe or Stew Hagen for a couple of days. Didn't even know about the downed cows.'

She sucked in her breath, then took a swallow of coffee.

'So Abe was setting you up.'

Travis looked steadily at her. 'I don't think he would've moved in on you if he'd been expecting me to come back alive.'

'What – what's he trying to do? Take over Thistle?'

'No. I think he and his bunch are trying to clean Thistle out this season. The mavericks are a good part of Dysart's regular income and with the count way down and the big herds' numbers slacked-off, Thistle would be in very bad shape.'

'Then – you think Abe was rustling steers as well as mavericks?'

'And not just from Thistle. Anders complained about the mavericks to Dysart but Lew Birch hinted others had been losing cattle as well. I've seen it before, places where the owner isn't on the spot and some smart aleck sees a way of cleaning him out in one slick move.'

She was silent for a time, poured herself another cup of coffee and sat down beside him with a small gasp. He had noticed how stiffly and awkwardly she moved.

'I should've killed McKinley,' he said. 'Now I've still got it to do.'

Abby's head came around sharply. 'You think he'll – oh, of course he will! You've marked up his face and body, the two things he was most proud of. Of course he'll want to kill you.'

'Yeah. So I'll take my sixgun if you'll dig it out from wherever you put it.'

She smiled. 'I just thought that one day you might feel you wanted to wear it again. What I found in the books was that Abe was running a racket with the men's pay. He was advancing them money against their wages and charging twenty per cent interest. He boasted about it to me – before – well – before he got off the subject.'

'Twenty per cent! Most of the crew wouldn't be able to afford to go paint the town red with McKinley collecting on their loans. Wouldn't be surprised to find he had other rackets going, too. Seems he aimed to grab every cent he could out of Thistle.'

She was silent for a time and then said quietly:

'Perhaps that's why they killed Ross.'

Travis's head snapped up. 'What?'

'Dysart told me he felt Ross had been murdered. He – Ross, that is, was not just put in as manager. He was an agent for the Cattlemen's Association. A range detective. Dysart's one of the commissioners of the Association. Other members, including Anders, have also been losing stock. So when the chance came to move in a new manager, Ross was given the job and orders to find out what was going on.'

He looked at her so hard that she dropped her gaze.

'You knew Ross, didn't you?'

'What makes you say that?'

'A few things I noticed before we arrived.'

'You must've been imagining things.' She stood abruptly and set down her empty cup, starting for the door. 'I must get out of this robe and into a proper dress before supper. I'll have a look at that wound on your chest then.'

'Fine. It's stiffening a little but Bud Corey washed it out with raw whiskey. If that don't kill any infection nothing will.'

'Bites by animals should never be neglected. Especially those who eat carrion. I'll clean it up with antiseptic when I'm dressed and bandage it properly. By the way – I'm ready for my first shooting lesson when you are.'

She smiled, blowing him a kiss, and went out.

His own smile slowly vanished as she closed the door behind her.

She had deliberately avoided saying whether she had known Ross or not. But he knew she had visited the man's grave in the small cemetery not far from the Thistle ranch house.

8

Oath of Vengeance

When Big Abe McKinley came round properly, he had to think hard for a few minutes, trying to figure out how the hell he had gotten here, to the cabin in the hideout canyon.

Once he tried to move he remembered.

Just working his mouth to cuss started pain all around the lower part of his face. Lifting a hand to feel caused him to groan aloud, knives of agony slashing under his arms and across his shoulders. He was spread-eagled face down and made growling noises in his throat until someone came into the room.

It was Stew Hagen who stood by the bunk looking down at the fallen giant.

'Best not try to talk, Abe. You been beat good. Face is a mess and like it or not you're gonna be scarred for life.'

That brought a roaring, deep-throated growl from Abe.

'Your back's a mess, flayed nigh to the

119

bone in places. You're gonna be sleepin' face down for quite a while. An' in case you don't 'member, it was Cody Travis done it to you. By the by, how's the weddin' tackle?'

Abe looked up with reddened eyes sunk deep in their bruised sockets. He made several mumbling noises, over and over, and Stew dropped to one knee, tilted his head close to the man's mashed lips so he could make out what he was saying. Just two words. Over and over.

'He's dead! He's dead! He's dead!'

'Yeah, well, we kinda figured that'd be your attitude, but we gotta move them mavericks out, Abe. Canyon's near full an' Stedmann'll be holdin' the pens for 'em in Butte. If you're right about Travis bein' an undercover agent for the Cattlemen's Association we gotta get them mavericks outta here pronto.'

Abe was all but snorting through his swollen nose with its blood-caked nostrils. He was glaring at Stew.

Hagen scratched at his left ear. 'Thing is, it's gonna take all the boys to move 'em down to Butte. Can't spare no one to leave with you, Abe...'

'Find – someone!' Abe grunted.

'Who? There's only five of us.'

'P – Patch – an' Chuck.'

Hagen arched his eyebrows. 'You said you weren't never gonna use them two again after–'

'Get – 'em. Kiley an' Wrango can stay with me.'

'Judas! The best riders!' Abe glared. Stew flushed.

'OK, if that's the way you want it. I'll send Race after Patch and Chuck right away–'

'You – go!' gasped Abe, just about spent from his efforts, sweat dribbling down his battered face, stinging the raw rope-wounds.

The room spun crazily and Abe collapsed, gasping, on the smelly bunk, groaning aloud. He had never been in such pain.

But it was nothing to what Mr and Mrs Cody Goddamn Travis had waiting for them!

No, sir!

The nearest town to Thistle was called Fort Hatfield although it had been many years since there had been any kind of fortification there. Truth was, a bunch of wolf-hunters and buffalo-runners had holed up in a large buffalo wallow when some of Red Cloud's braves were tearing up any part of the country that had held the footprint of a

121

white man. The trapped hunters built a square wall five feet high and two feet thick out of mud and stone from the nearby Old Squaw Creek and managed to hold off a couple of hundred Indians until a cavalry patrol came to their rescue.

The campsite had become known as Fort Hatfield, the name being that of the buffalo hunter who had first suggested building the wall. It had grown into a small town.

Cody Travis didn't think much of the place, a handful of scattered log or clapboard buildings, meandering main street and side-alleys, weed-grown mostly, with a tree here and there. Old Squaw Creek ran diagonally through the town and there was a short wooden bridge crossing it near the law office. Travis dismounted outside the weather-blackened building, left his roan's reins dangling over the hitch rail and went inside.

He hoped this wouldn't take long. There was a hell of a lot of work to be done on Thistle and he was shorthanded now he had fired Abe and his hardcases. And he didn't like being away from Abby although she was recovering well enough. Too bad she couldn't handle guns very well. Her first shooting lessons had been dismal affairs, but she'd taken it well enough, said she'd just have to find some other way of protecting herself. He had sent a couple of hands out to the pasture where he had killed the bear to skin the animal so it could be made into a rug. Brighten things up for her a little.

Lew Birch sat huddled close to a small potbelly stove in one corner of the untidy office. He was puffing on a pipe, his head wreathed in tobacco smoke. He waved it clear as Cody came in, taking off his hat.

'Feeling the cold?'

'At my age it ain't cold that matters so much as rheumatics. Heat keeps your joints in workin' order. Sit.'

Travis sat down a few feet to one side and rolled a cigarette.

'Kid rode out and said you wanted to see me.'

'Yeah. You come upriver on the *Miss Caroline*, din' you?'

Travis nodded, feeling a slight tension, as he fired up his cigarette.

'Just as far as Pierce's Landing. Cut across country for Abby's benefit. She's never been this far north before.'

Birch nodded. 'Been two bodies washed ashore south of the Landin'. Looked like they'd died violently.'

Travis waited, saying nothing.

'They couldn'ta been pretty after a couple weeks in the river. Kind of glad it weren't me found 'em.'

The lawman waited now and Travis tried to show interest.

'Where we going with this, Sheriff?'

'I ain't sure. Guess I'm kinda bored in this job. Too old for anythin' else, though. But I like a mystery and I was wonderin' if you might of seen these fellers on the steamer. It's taken the marshal a time to track down all the passengers but you'd likely recall if you met 'em, I guess.'

'Could've, if you're sure they were on the boat.'

'Oh, yeah. Ain't no mistakin' a body that's fallen – or was pushed – into a paddle wheel. Just like a piece of jelly, most every bone broke or chewed up. Flop, flop, flop...'

Travis kept his face blank. Birch gestured to his desk.

'Top drawer, right-hand side. Manila folder with a rough drawin' of a paddle-wheeler on it. I like to doodle when I'm thinkin' – take a look.'

Travis got the folder and brought it back. He opened it as he sat down again.

There were several papers. The letter from

the marshal who had found the bodies, another paper describing how they most likely looked before mutilation and a couple of weeks in the river. Travis recognized them as the men who had jumped him on the riverboat.

'Think I might've seen them, but it's only a general description. Could fit a lot of men.'

'Well, yeah, but there's some old bodyscars mentioned which you wouldn't've seen and they helped identify 'em for sure. See the last page.'

Travis read out the possible names of the dead men.

'Smoke Landers and Arch – Satterfield?' Cody snapped his head up at the last name. 'Any kin to...?'

'Yeah, brother to Race. Fact is, both men worked for Thistle not long before you showed up. But there was some kinda hassle and Ross fired 'em. Pair of real hardcases.'

'And they showed up on the riverboat I was taking up here...'

Birch leaned towards him, the old eyes hard and searching.

'So you *did* see 'em on the *Miss Caroline*?'

Travis nodded, holding the man's gaze.

'I won eighty bucks at faro. Went out on to

the rear deck to smoke a cheroot and think about how I was gonna spend it. They jumped me. It got real nasty real fast. One fell into the paddle-wheel, the other – well, we tangled and I threw him over the side. Pretty sure it was these two.' He tapped the page.

'And you never reported it.'

'Matter of fact I mentioned it to the captain on the quiet and he asked me to keep it to myself. Said it wouldn't do his boat much good if folk thought there were men sailing on her ready to jump any man who won a stake at gambling.'

Lew Birch nodded gently. 'That's what you thought it was? Couple of thugs after your eighty bucks?'

'Yeah, that's what I thought at the time.'

'Now...?'

'Well – if they'd worked for Thistle and one was Race Satterfield's brother, seems like something of a coincidence, don't it?'

'I get me a uncomfortable feelin' about coincidences like that.'

'So do I. But why would they jump me if it wasn't for the money?'

'You said it got real nasty right off.'

Travis nodded. 'Yeah, I reckoned they aimed to kill me – but why? Unless – it had something to do with the mavericks.' He waited, but although Birch's eyes narrowed the old sheriff didn't say anything. 'I suspect McKinley and some of the others are branding mavericks, both from Thistle and from other ranches, and selling them on the side. Dysart does too.'

'Common enough racket on isolated spreads like Thistle.' Birch's voice was grating now.

Travis studied the end of his burning cigarette.

'Yeah. Works best if the local law's ... involved. And almost always the cattle agent.'

'That'd be Otis Stedmann over to Butte,' Lew Birch said heavily. 'Notice you're wearin' a sixgun, Travis. If you think that gives you the gall to come in here and accuse me of graft, I'm here to tell you that I can still outdraw 'most any man in Montana Territory.'

'Well, I don't aim to put you to the test, Birch, unless you push it. But you don't know much about me. I might just be the one you can't beat to the draw.'

Lew Birch threw a little more wood on the stove, spoke without looking round as he closed the door.

'You had no call to say what you did.'

'Was just thinking out loud. Nothing personal in it. But if those hardcases *had* been sent to stop me coming here, it seems that whatever racket is going on is a lot bigger than I thought.'

'Well, I guess Thistle is big enough to stand the loss of a few mavericks, tho' I s'pose that ain't the real point. By the by, hear you did somethin' no one else has managed to do: you beat up Abe McKinley.'

'He had it coming.'

'Thought you might've killed him.'

'Me, too.'

Birch tapped out his pipe and blew through the stem.

'You're a surprise to a lot of folk, Travis. But that won't stop you goin' down to a bullet you don't see comin'.'

'That a threat?'

Birch sighed. 'No, damnit! I'm just warnin' you in case you think you're ten feet tall and bullet-proof now you kicked Big Abe in the balls. He ain't a man to forget.'

'Nor am I.' Travis stood. 'Look, I've got to find some men to replace the ones I fired with McKinley. What happens about these bodies they fished out of the river? Am I in any trouble?'

'Hell, I dunno – *I'm* satisfied. I believe you

... solved the mystery, you might say. Let the marshal figure things out for himself. Them bits of crowbait ain't no loss.'

'Thanks, Birch.' As Travis turned to leave the lawman said:

'Dysart mention the Cattlemen's Association at all?'

Travis paused with his hand on the door handle, frowning slightly.

'Might've, in passing. Why?'

'Well, if he'd hired you to look into rustlin' up here for the Association, puttin' you in as manager as a cover would be a smart move...'

He paused and let the rest trail off.

Travis smiled faintly. 'Be a good reason for someone to send those hardcases to see I didn't get off that riverboat alive, I guess.'

Birch looked expectant, but Travis merely opened the door. The sheriff's face straightened.

'Mighty powerful, that Cattlemen's Association.'

Travis nodded. 'So I hear.' Then he went out on to the boardwalk.

The sheriff kicked at the door on the stove, savagely.

It hadn't worked! He still didn't know if Travis was an Association range detective or not!

'Goddamn, close-mouthed reformed drunk!' he said aloud, bitterly.

There was a bunch of men with their feet up around the cracker barrel in the general store. Some had the look of range men about them. All looked steadily at Cody Travis as he came in. He nodded genially enough, the storekeeper murmuring a 'Howdy, mister.'

'I'm Cody Travis, manager of the Thistle spread. I need six top hands and I need 'em now. Forty-and-found, guaranteed a dry, warm bunk and good grub. Sundays off on a rotating basis to give every man one free Sunday each month. If there's a wrangler among you, he gets extra pay for busting broncs and I'm authorized to offer a bonus after the trail drive. How much depends on what price we get for the cows. Any takers?'

Some men looked interested but quickly composed their faces again, shook their heads.

'No takers at all?' Travis was surprised.

'Well, I'm gettin' a mite tired of supplyin' soda dodgers to a bunch of loafers, I declare,' spoke up the storekeeper but the men laughed at him, gave him a hard time with jokes about his miserliness. The man subsided quickly, muttering.

But no one wanted a job, although Travis was sure two rannies came close to accepting, but sharp nudges from nearby companions kept them silent.

'OK, fellers. Think about it. I'll look in again before I quit town.'

'Save yourself the trouble, mister,' spoke up someone in the centre of the group. 'You ain't gonna get no hands for Thistle here.'

Travis didn't push it. He went to the saloon halfway down the block, a ramshackle place with broken boards roughly patched, one window with rags stuffed in a large bullet-hole, the frame splintered. Inside it was mighty smoky and reeked of rotgut whiskey, spilled beer, stale sweat and the redolent odour of men who rode horses for a living.

Travis climbed up onto a table and got their attention, gave his spiel about what a fine place Thistle was to work. Most of the men turned back to their drinks, not listening. Again he saw a couple of obvious range men riding the grubline who looked interested but they didn't accept. He followed the gaze of one of these and began to understand.

Stew Hagen lounged on the half-wrecked,

131

silent piano, glass of beer in hand, flanked by a couple of rough-looking *hombres* who were watching him closely. Travis climbed down from the table and started towards Hagen. The man on his left, lean, mean and gun-hung, stepped forward to meet the rancher, left hand raised, palm out.

'Far enough, Travis.'

Travis stopped. 'Who're you?'

'Name's Chuck Farraday. Why don't you go on back to this Thistle while you can? Save everyone a heap of trouble. You ain't hirin' no cowhands today.'

There was a taut silence in the smoky room now, all attention focused on the corner where the piano stood drunkenly. The man still standing beside Hagen wore twin guns and he had his bony hands resting on the butts now. Travis shifted his gaze to Hagen.

'Your doing, Stew?'

Hagen shrugged, smiling crookedly, lifting one hand in a vague gesture.

'I'm just mindin' my own business and havin' a drink. Say, Travis! How'd *you* like a drink? Teach there behind the bar makes his own redeye and it's guaranteed to drill you an extra asshole. Like a glass?'

'No, thanks. But then I wouldn't drink

with a snake like you anyway, Hagen.'

The smile dropped from Stew's face. 'Well, I guess you bein' a drunk an' all you'd know all about snakes, wouldn't you? Pink ones? Candy-striped...? Dancin' the polka on the ceilin'...?'

That got laughter from the drinkers and even brought a half-smile to Travis's face.

'Stew, you're a real stupid son of a bitch, you know that?'

A lot of men weren't sure just what happened next. The insult brought Hagen to his toes. The twin-gun man stepped forward threateningly, but that was only to drag Travis's attention away from Chuck Farraday.

Travis didn't fall for it.

Chuck went for his gun, hand slapping audibly against the butt. Travis set a deadly stare on the man and said flatly:

'You're about to die, Chuck, if you lift that gun out of leather!'

Chuck hesitated, then curled a lip and mouthed a curse, lifting the sixgun. There was the thunder of a single shot and Chuck Farraday did die where he stood. Only he wasn't standing for long. Travis's slug flung him back into a table, scattering chairs, falling off the edge and bringing down the bottles and glasses there, sending the men who had been seated ducking for cover.

The twin-gun man's jaw was slack with shock and he let his half-drawn guns fall back into leather, quickly lifting his hands shoulder high. Travis put a bullet through the right one and the man howled, snatched the hand against his chest, staggering into the piano, which made a tinny, ringing noise even as the wounded man dropped to his knees, sobbing.

The smoking gun-barrel was now covering Stew Hagen who swallowed, started to lift his hands, glanced down at his moaning companion, and then folded them quickly across his chest.

'Abe send you in? Here, and down at the store?' Travis asked and Hagen swallowed, licked his lips and nodded. 'Any message?'

'Just – just said you better get used to workin' Thistle short-handed.'

'Uh-huh. Well, I've got a message for Abe.' Travis stepped forward and gunwhipped Hagen to his knees. The man swayed there, one hand on the filthy floor supporting him, blood dribbling from two deep cuts on the side of his head.

'Tell Abe that Old Sam Colt was right: his guns are great equalizers. And any time

Abe's feeling more than equal to the task, I'll meet him anywhere on his terms and prove it.'

He placed a boot against Stew's chest and kicked the man flat on his back.

The batwings slapped open and Sheriff Lew Birch came in, a sawed-off shotgun in his hands. His rheumy eyes went straight to Travis.

'See you're keepin' in practice.'

'It was kind of forced on me, Sheriff.' Travis had holstered his gun now and ran his eyes over the staring men. 'Anyone int'rested in working for Thistle now...?'

He was surprised at how many shuffled forward.

9

Range War

The two men the new ramrod, Bud Corey, had sent to skin the bear were Jack Woodring and a man whose name was the same as that of a governor of Texas but who went by the handle of Pecos. Both were lean, hard Texans, Woodring taller than Pecos, who was thin as a reed.

They were experienced cowboys, had shaken Travis by the hand after he had fired Abe McKinley and his bunch.

'Them sonuvers were like to rob this ranch blind,' Pecos had said. 'We seen it happenin' but we was wonderin' who we could trust to tell about it.'

Travis had frowned at that. 'I can savvy you not being too sure about me, but what about Lew Birch?'

Both men had looked uncomfortable and finally Jack Woodring said, 'Heard talk.'

That was all he would say and Travis had used it as the basis for his veiled accusation in the sheriff's office in Fort Hatfield. Just testing the air – but it hadn't produced any real result.

The men had sweated over the bear hide and figured Travis was lucky some wolf hadn't found the corpse during the night and chewed a hunk out of it. There had been some scavenger activity but only on the cows. Maybe the wolves or mountain lions preferred beef to bear-meat.

The men spread the hide flesh side up, pegged it enough to hold it reasonably taut and scraped off the bits of flesh and gristle still adhering to it, using the flat of their knives.

'Gonna make a pretty good rug,' opined Pecos.

'Once he repairs the hole in the back of the head. Tough feller, that Travis. Don't look much, on the quiet side, but any man who'd fight off a bear this size, then kick big Abe where he lives is OK in my book.'

'Yeah. He's better than Ross, I reckon.'

They rolled cigarettes and discussed the new manager a little more. Then they froze as three riders suddenly appeared out of the brush, rifles levelled at them. They jumped to their feet, recognizing the men. Wrango, Kiley and Southpaw. The three meanest of

Abe's bunch.

'Well, what we got here?' Kiley said, heeling his mount forward. The other two spread out and covered the Texans. 'Two of the goody-goody boys, doin' just like they was told.'

'Best way to be, Kile,' allowed Southpaw but Wrango shook his head, spitting.

'Hell it is. Makes life borin'.' He suddenly jumped his mount forward and slid a boot free of the stirrup, kicking Pecos in the side of the head.

The Texan stumbled and fell to one knee. Kiley leaned out of the saddle and rapped him good across the head with his rifle barrel. Moaning, Pecos spread out, almost unconscious. Jack Woodring made a move for his sixgun which was hanging on a low treebranch a few feet away. Wrango jumped his mount into him, knocking him sprawling against the tree. Jack clawed for support, sliding down.

By then Wrango was out of the saddle, rifle sheathed, big fists doubling. He slammed Jack in the ribs as the lean man straightened, pushing him back against the tree. Woodring's boots slipped on the tree roots and he stumbled into Wrango, arms going about the man's waist. Wrango tried to knee him in the

138

face but Jack butted him hard in the midriff, straightened and got one through the rustler's guard. Blood spurted from Wrango's nose and Jack bared his teeth as he moved in.

But Southpaw slugged him with his rifle and drove him to his knees. Wrango, staring at the blood on his hand, spat, swore, and moved in kicking and punching, ramming Jack's body against the tree, boots slamming again and again into his ribs.

Jack groaned and desperately tried to get up but Southpaw and Kiley grabbed his arms, hauled him upright and spread him against the tree.

Wrango grinned through the blood smearing his mouth, spread his feet for purchase and began slugging methodically, each blow lifting Jack's boots a couple of inches off the ground. Wrango grunted with the effort.

When he was winded and gasping for breath, Southpaw and Kiley let Jack fall. The lean Texan was almost unrecognizable beneath the blood and torn flesh.

When he could breathe more easily, Wrango started on the huddled unconscious form again, kicking Jack's limp body half-way across the clearing.

He moved in on the battered man, grinning tightly.

It was dark when Cody Travis arrived back from town with the new men. He found Abby working over Jack. Pecos, who had received a gunwhipping from Kiley and Southpaw, looked sick as he sat nursing a cup of coffee, head bandaged, face bruised and battered.

He told Travis that they had sent Jack home wrapped in the bearskin, himself roped to his saddle, bleeding.

'You brought him back, Pecos. That's what counts.' Cody walked over and looked down at Woodring. 'He gonna make it?' he asked his wife tautly.

'I – don't rightly know, Cody. He's taken a terrible beating.'

Travis swung towards Pecos. 'Which one did it?'

'Wrango. He went plumb loco after Jack busted his nose. Said to tell you that's what'll happen to any man who rides for Thistle and comes up into the Beaverheads beyond Skillet Crick.'

Travis nodded gently, glancing at Abby.

'Trying to keep us out. We saw Stew Hagen way back in there, remember? I took a look but lost his trail. Still, I reckon we look hard enough we'll find where they've been branding the mavericks.'

'They'll kill someone, Cody,' Pecos said, thickened lips and cut tongue and missing teeth making some of his words difficult to understand. 'They're a mean bunch and once Abe's up and around again–'

'Big *hombre* like him won't take long to recover,' Travis allowed. 'So – best do what has to be done before I've got him to tangle with again, I guess.'

Abby came around fast, frowning at her husband.

'Just what does that mean?'

'Wrango beat up on two of my men going about their business, Abby. He has to answer for that.'

She wrung out a bloody rag, soaked it in clean water and laid it gently over the badly torn forehead of the unconscious Woodring.

'They're smart, or cunning enough to know you'll do exactly what you're thinking, Cody! You'll be riding into a trap.'

'Reckon that's what they've got in mind, but I'll be expecting it, so I'll take precautions.'

'Don't be so foolish!' Abby snapped. 'You can't do this alone!' By now she knew better than to try to talk him out of such action completely – she had learnt his strict code and just how stubborn he could be – but she *could* try to get him to consider some help.

'I'll be able to ride by noon tomorrow,' offered Pecos. Travis shook his head and Abby paled.

'My chore, Pecos. I'll need to tell the new men I've hired. They have to know what they're taking on.' He flicked his gaze to Abby. 'Managed to get eight volunteers, eventually.'

'I'm not sure I like that "eventually", Cody!'

He smiled faintly. 'All been ironed out with Lew Birch. I'll start first thing in the morning. Be full dark pretty soon.'

'Cody,' she said as he opened the door. 'I – think a doctor should see Jack. There are broken bones in his face and I fear a rib has splintered and perhaps pierced a lung.'

'All right. Kettle and Hondo can take him into town in the buckboard.' He left to go to the bunkhouse.

While Kettle and Hondo hurriedly finished their supper, Travis told the new hands about Jack's beating. Only one man, name of Starbuck, said he didn't want the job.

Turning his hat awkwardly in his hands he told Cody, 'I figured Big Abe was out of it now. I've tangled with him before and I got no notion to do it again. Sorry, Mr Travis.'

Cody nodded. 'Fair enough. Anyone else?'

One of the others, a young, rangy cowpoke, licked his lips and said he thought he might ride out with Starbuck. He didn't like the sounds of this Big Abe McKinley.

Travis paid them five dollars each and they said they would ride along when the buckboard left for town with Jack Woodring.

Travis was surprised to see Abby hurrying down from the ranch house, her small carpetbag in hand, a scarf tied around her head.

'I'd better ride in the back with Jack, Cody,' she said worriedly 'The motion just might force that broken rib right through his lung and–'

'Whatever you think best, Abby.' He kissed her.

She clung to his arms, looking up into his face.

'Be careful, Cody. I'd much rather Lew Birch did this...'

'It's my chore, Abby.'

She nodded resignedly, turning quickly towards the buckboard where Kettle helped her up into the back and then climbed up beside Hondo who had the reins.

Travis was glad to see Kettle take his rifle from under the seat, lever in a shell and sit with it across his knees as the buckboard drove out of the dark yard, Starbuck and the young ranny following.

'Should've killed both the sons of bitches!' growled Abe McKinley, after learning about the beating handed out to Jack Woodring's and Pecos's gun whipping. His face looked terrible, flaking with raw flesh and shrivelled skin on the way to becoming scabs. He still couldn't move his facial muscles very well and his speech was slurred.

He was sitting up now but only for short periods, afraid to rest his flayed back against anything that wasn't as soft as a cloud. He glared at Wrango, Kiley and Southpaw.

'The three of you should've done it! Told you to teach 'em a damn lesson Travis'd never forget!'

'We din' think you'd want any more killin', after Ross, Abe,' Wrango said. 'Birch weren't happy about that and he said–'

'The hell with Birch! I'm pullin' out all stops from here on in,' cut in Abe sourly. 'Mebbe you did right after all – I want

144

Travis for myself! I aim to break him in two and make sure he feels every goddamn second of it!'

'Well, he'll come after us, sure as shootin',' Kiley said, hoping to keep Abe from getting too riled. 'When he sees what Wrango done to Jack Woodring, he'll froth at the mouth.'

McKinley glared, then slowly nodded. 'Yeah. Seems he's tougher and faster on the draw than we figured. I mean, Chuck was no slouch and Patch ain't usually scared so easy ... or so he says!' Big Abe glared at Patchett, the man who had backed down in front of Travis, right hand now bandaged.

'You wasn't there, Abe. Ask Stew how fast Travis was!' Patch said, but Abe was already thinking of something else. He nodded, coming to a decision.

'All right. Wrango, you go back to where you worked over Jack and leave some tracks into the hills. But not in this direction.'

Wrango frowned. 'Where then?'

'Just lead him deep into the hills. Towards that old line shack of Horseshoe's oughta do. They ain't used it all winter and it's still empty.'

Wrango nodded: it sounded better to him now that he knew he would have a cosy line shack to wait in – it still got mighty cold in the Beaverheads.

'I wait and pick Travis off as he comes in, that it, Abe?' he asked.

He was surprised – and so were the others – when Abe McKinley shook his head slowly. 'No, that ain't it at all...'

They fell silent as he told them just what he had in mind.

Abe glared. 'This is war now, nothin' else. Travis asked for it and I'm gonna see he gets it. Right in the neck!'

The doctor was pleased with the treatment that Abby had given Jack Woodring, especially the way she had taken the precaution of strapping up his ribs.

'It's certain he's got at least two broken ribs and I can clearly hear a splintered end grating,' the medic added. 'If those jagged ends pierce his lungs...'

He didn't bother completing the sentence. Abby knew full well the implications of such a thing happening. Kettle and Hondo were waiting outside for news of their saddlemate and after Abby had helped the doctor as much as she could, she went outside to tell them about Jack's condition.

They stood quickly as she entered the room.

'I'm afraid the news isn't the best, boys. But he's in good hands with the doctor and if anyone can pull him through, he's the man to do it.'

Kettle and Hondo exchanged glances and the latter cleared his throat.

'We'd kinda like to – hang around, ma'am, if that's OK.'

Abby frowned. 'Well, I understand your concern but there's really nothing to be gained by your waiting here. But – it's a long drive back to Thistle and it will be daylight soon. I have no objection to your staying over until the morning.'

They gave her brief smiles and thanked her. As they turned to leave she asked if they would notify Sheriff Birch about what had happened, then she returned to see what else she could do to help the hard-working doctor.

Lew Birch arrived shortly afterwards, shirt only half-tucked into his trousers and crookedly buttoned. But his sixgun sat firmly enough in its usual place on his thigh.

At the doctor's nod, Abby went into the waiting-room with the lawman.

'I need more details than Kettle and Hondo gave me,' Birch said without pre-amble.

'All I can tell you is that Cody sent Jack and Pecos to skin a bear he'd killed and they were set upon by three of McKinley's hardcases. Wrango, Kiley and Southpaw. Pecos was gunwhipped but Jack was beaten – very badly, *very* badly, Sheriff, by Wrango.'

'He didn't look too good.'

'I don't think he'll make it through the night. Wrango apparently used his boots – freely.'

Birch's thin lips moved in a silent curse and his old eyes narrowed.

'Where's Cody?'

'Back at the ranch.' Abby spoke in clipped tones that brought an alertness to the lawman's face.

He knew she wasn't lying, but she wasn't telling him everything, either.

'He waitin' to see if Jack makes it or not?'

'All I know is he stayed behind at the ranch.'

'Uh-huh. Mrs Travis, I know your husband's reputation as a town-tamin' lawman years ago, before he hit the booze. He was one tough *hombre* and I've seen signs not too long back that he's recovered – and that he's *still* mighty tough, even though he seems a lot quieter.'

He waited expectantly but although Abby

looked politely interested she said nothing. Birch sighed.

'Mrs Travis, I have to ask you this: is your husband working for the Cattlemen's Association?'

Abby stiffened, frowned, lifting her gaze to the sheriff's face.

'He was employed by Jock Dysart.'

Birch nodded. 'Who happens to be one of the commissioners of the Association and who is havin' rustlin' problems right now.'

'Then he's probably made his own ... arrangements with the Association.'

The sheriff sighed. 'Ma'am, I have it on good authority that the Association has put an undercover agent in here to look into the rustling and general range conditions. I think Cody Travis is their man, and I feel – slighted. *I'm* the local law and I should've been contacted by way of courtesy if nothin' else. Whoever this agent is, sooner or later he's gonna want my co-operation and I'd like to be ready, know who I'm dealin' with. You can see that, can't you?'

'My profession is nursing, Sheriff. I believe I can understand what you're saying, but I can still only tell you that Cody was hired by Mr Dysart. He's my husband but he doesn't discuss his professional details

149

with me, no more than he expects me to discuss mine.'

Birch's face coloured but he got himself quickly under control. He glanced towards the door behind which Jack Woodring was fighting for his life.

'I hope you'll be good enough to let me know if Jack don't make it! Now *that* ain't askin' you to betray any blamed, misplaced ethics, I hope!'

He wheeled and went out into the night, Abby's teeth tugging at her lower lip as she watched the door close behind him.

10

Live Bait

There was something wrong with the tracks.

It was barely daylight but Travis had good eyes and he noticed something different about the tracks he was following. He couldn't put his finger on it right away.

The site where the bear had been skinned and the dead cows lay was half a mile behind him now. Predators and scavengers squabbled over the rotting meat but they scattered reluctantly while he scouted for sign. He had always made a practice of noting the tracks made by the horse most favoured by any man he was riding with. That way if the man went missing from a trail drive or round-up in dangerous country he knew right away who it was, even what the horse was likely to do if it had lost its rider: come home, run off or stay put.

At Thistle he had taken careful note of the tracks left by the mounts used by Abe McKinley and his bunch of hardcases. Wrango forked a smoke gelding that had a way of flinging the left forefoot out before placing it on the ground. This made a distinctive track as the hoof always came down in a toe-first slide from the left.

So Wrango's tracks were easy enough to single out. The sign left by Southpaw's and Kiley's was different enough so he could name which set belonged to which rider. But Wrango was the one he was interested in.

Then, as the sunlight strengthened, he saw what was bothering him: there were *two* sets of tracks made by Wrango's mount. Same horse, same hoofmark, but one lot was older. This would be the original set left after Jack and Pecos had been beaten. Travis had come far enough to know that the men had ridden into the Beaverheads and, he suspected, headed for a hideout in the general area where he and Abby had seen Stew Hagen.

But now the fresher tracks made by Wrango angled away from the others – and they were much less then twenty-four hours old. There had been a sloppy attempt to cover Wrango's original trail to make it look as if the other two had gone on without him.

But why in hell would Wrango come back here

and lay a new set of tracks, separating from Kiley and Southpaw?

Easy enough to figure: they *wanted* Travis to follow the fresher set. It would be reasonable to expect Wrango to clear the country after the brutal beating he had dished out to Jack Woodring. And they knew Travis well enough by now to know the man would go after Wrango...

Wrango was the bait in a trap already set! For him!

Travis stood up slowly now, hand resting on his sixgun butt.

Somewhere out there, maybe behind, maybe off to one side paralleling Wrango's trail, or already in an ambush position ahead, waiting for Wrango to lead Travis into his sights, would be another of Abe's hardcases. Rifle ready, itchy finger on the trigger, ready to put a bullet into Travis's back.

He smiled thinly.

'Not today, fellers,' he said aloud. He climbed into the saddle and rode off along the treacherous trail with loaded rifle across his knees. 'Not today.'

Wrango was uneasy. He wasn't afraid of Travis but he *was* leery of him. He respected no man, but he walked mighty careful around anyone who could put someone like Big Abe out of action.

The trap *should* work. The trail he had left was plain enough, yet not so easy to read that Travis would suspect anything. *He hoped!*

Kiley was a good shot and he sure had no love for Travis. Anyway, he only had to wing him...

Still, Wrango felt edgy and kept looking around as he climbed deeper into the hills.

He suddenly laughed. A short, loud sound that triggered a wave of relief flooding through his body. *There it was!* Anders' line camp, quiet as a grave in the backwoods, but a lot emptier. Most of the gear had been looted by grub-liners long since – hell, someone had even taken the potbelly stove! But there was a small open fireplace and Wrango didn't mind the chore of chopping a couple of armfuls of wood so he could sleep warm. Last time he was here there was still one bunk more or less intact, but most of the cupboards were gone, having been ripped apart by drifters and fed into the potbelly when it was operating.

He glanced up at the sky. Past noon, he figured, and black-edged thunderheads were just touching the sawtooth ridges in the north. It would be a cold wet night, so he figured to dump his war bag and go cut some wood before the rain started.

He tossed his war bag and bedroll in through the door, had a quick look for snakes or packrats, saw only a few spiders in the corners. He took his tomahawk out of his saddle-bag went around to the rear, where he tethered his horse in the timber, then collected a bunch of deadfalls and commenced to cut them into manageable size. He rammed the tomahawk through his trouser belt, piled up his arms so he could just barely see over the load of wood and whistled softly as he plodded back to the front where the only entrance was. He stumbled on the stoop, staggered across the gritty, dusty floor – and reared to a dead stop, jaw sagging in disbelief.

Cody Travis sat gingerly on the edge of the one remaining bunk, his rifle held loosely, but pointed in the general direction of Wrango's heavy belly.

'Thanks, Wrango. Just what I need to keep me warm tonight. Put it down there on the flagstones in front of the fireplace. Mighty careful.'

The rifle barrel whipped into line with

Wrango's right knee. His breath hissing through his yellowed teeth, heart pounding, he walked to the hearth and dumped the load of deadwood.

He used the noise and the motion to screen his right hand sliding the tomahawk free of his belt. His thick arm swept up and back – and then Travis's rifle went off like a thunderclap inside the musty old line shack. Wrango's right leg kicked out from under him and he collapsed, face contorted as he screamed, the small axe striking sparks from the flagstones as it skidded across the floor.

Wrango writhed and rolled about, clutching his bloody knee-cap, splintered bone stabbing his fingers. He sobbed and retched with the pain. Travis watched, deadpan, the rifle muzzle still pointed at the big man.

Wrango's ugly face was grey, already drawn with extreme pain. He slowly subsided, making great gasps mixed with involuntary sobs. His eyes were red and streaming. He had bitten deeply into his bottom lip and blood dripped from his stubbled jaw.

'Brought that on yourself, Wrango. Didn't aim to cripple you up right away, but now you got a taste of what's waiting for you if you don't answer my questions.'

Wrango managed to twist his blood-streaked mouth and grit out several obscenities. Travis said nothing, slowly raised the rifle and drew a bead on Wrango's other knee. The man shuddered and fell back, gasping.

'Don't!' he croaked. 'I – I've had enough!'

'Hell, you give up easy,' Travis said without lowering the rifle. 'Figured you'd make for here. Bud Corey told me about this line camp. I figured mebbe you and Abe's men were using it as headquarters for rustling. See I was wrong about that, but I got here ahead of you, saw you coming, and slipped inside while you were cutting wood.'

Wrango didn't have enough steam left to curse. He said wearily, words all slurred by the pain that was now overwhelming him. 'Wha'yawan...?'

'A few answers. Like, where've you got the mavericks stashed? When're you moving 'em out and where to? I figure it's to Butte where Otis Stedmann is waiting to ship 'em out for the railhead mixed in with legitimate herds. Once they're on his waybill, no one's gonna query where they came from. Even if they do, he'll tell them to wire Lew Birch, the local law, and Birch'll wire back that sure, the cows are from a local ranch that's

157

been here for years. Legitimate as hell.'

Wrango stared. 'How'd you...?' He paused, still breathless. 'You're guessin'!'

Travis smiled wryly. 'But a pretty good guess, eh?'

'Abe said all along you was workin' for the Cattlemen's Association!'

Travis said nothing but seemed surprised at being charged with being an undercover agent.

'What I want from you right now, Wrango, is for you to tell me where those cows are. So start talking.'

'You'll – get – nothin' outta – *me!*' gasped Wrango as a new wave of pain surged through him. He collapsed on his face, writhing again, sick and close to passing out.

'Well, you might be tough enough, Wrango, but I'll have to make sure. So here goes your other knee.'

Wrango screamed. Not anything intelligible, just a blood-chilling cry of anticipated agony wrenched from him as he heard Travis cock the rifle's hammer. Cody waited.

'*Don't!*' Wrango croaked desperately. 'Don' shoo' me! I'll tell you – everythin'!'

'Why, you gutless son of a bitch!'

The door crashed open under a driving riding-boot and hard on the words of disgust came the crack of a rifle, and again. The two bullets hammered into Wrango and flung his heavy body half-way into the fireplace, a fog of old ash rising about him.

By then Travis was diving for the floor, rifle thrust out in front, the barrel riding high with recoil as he triggered. He glimpsed the man in the doorway, recognized Kiley, and saw him reel as the bullet gouged his side.

Kiley's smoking rifle swung towards Travis's rolling figure, blasted, the bullet going wild, ploughing into the bunk frame. As he rolled, Cody Travis worked the rifle lever, fired across his body.

Door-frame splinters stung Kiley's face. The man stumbled deeper into the cabin but managed to stay on his feet. He set his boots wide and braced the rifle butt into his hip, working lever and trigger, raking Travis's corner with hammering lead. Travis skidded, started to rise to one knee, but was knocked sprawling, head jerking back, hat flying. He spun on to his belly as his vision blurred. He lined up the Winchester muzzle on Kiley's chest.

Kiley was flung back against the wall. Travis levered a fresh load into the breech and put another shot into the rustler as he began to topple forward. The lead spun him away and Kiley dropped his rifle, clawed at the wall and fell in a huddle, kicking twice before being still.

On one knee now, sagging a little, Travis levered in a fresh cartridge, wondering why the hell it took so long, why the lever seemed so stiff.

Then he felt the hot, thick blood flooding across his forehead, crawling into his eyes and blinding him as the first wave of real pain hit him like a kick from a Mexican mule.

He went down and out, as quickly as a man could snap his fingers.

Abby brought the bad news to Lew Birch just before daylight.

'Jack died ten minutes ago, Sheriff,' she told him wearily. 'He didn't regain consciousness.'

Lew Birch, sleepy, came wide awake, his grey stubble standing straight out from his leathery flesh as he clamped his jaws tightly.

'Goddamn Abe!' he gritted, the words barely audible.

Abby heard them, frowned a little, but before she could speak, the sheriff said:

'Thanks for lettin' me know, Mrs Travis. I'll take it from here. 'Mornin' to you, ma'am.'

He closed the door gently. Abby stood there a few moments, then turned and hurried away.

Birch dressed quickly, shivered and spluttered as he splashed cold water on his face and then strapped on his sixgun, slid it from the holster and checked the loads. He took down a carbine, changed his mind and chose a rifle instead – its tubular magazine held eleven cartridges against the carbine's seven. Being able to get off a few extra rounds without pausing to reload could make a difference – the difference between living and dying.

He kicked the livery man awake and told him to get his mount saddled pronto. While the sleepy, complaining man obeyed, Birch crossed the street, banged on the door of the general store, and bullied Jason the storekeeper into packing him a grubsack with vittles enough for three days.

When Lew Birch rode out of town, spurring his big roan stallion, it was barely ten minutes since Abby had brought him the news of Jack's death.

He rode hard for the hills, cutting across

country from the town to the part of the Beaverheads where he knew Abe McKinley and his men had their hideout.

'I *told* that son of a bitch, after Ross, *no more killin'!*' Birch gritted aloud, the rain-laden wind whipping the words back into his throat. 'Hell, we already got the Cattlemen's Association's agent prowlin' around. Next thing they'll send in a US marshal. It's time I had it out proper with Abe, anyways ... time I – got a little dignity back into my life.'

There was a hint of a whine of self-pity in the words and he angrily cleared his throat. *Damnit! If Travis, a reformed drunk, could prick his conscience this way, he ought to be able to summon up a little pride and enough guts to take his chances the way the cards were dealt...*

He sat straighter in the saddle; he was too short to say he rode 'tall in the saddle', but for a small man he managed to look solid and determined as he spurred the roan into the first of the foothills.

He paused on a ledge to pack a pipe, thought better of it, because it was a damn nuisance trying to keep it going while riding, and put it back into his shirt pocket.

That was when he glimpsed the movement below through the trees. A flash of

162

colour down there!

'By Godfrey! Someone's followin' me!'

His old heart banged against his ribs as he slid the rifle out of the saddle scabbard. He was in no mood for this! He wouldn't kill whoever it was but he'd damn soon shoot the horse out from under him. Then let the sonuver find his own way back to town. It would take him the rest of the day on foot. Teach the nosy bastard a lesson.

But first, maybe he'd find out what he was up to, following him into the hills. And unless he got the right answers, the sonuver wouldn't be walking anywhere!

Sheriff Birch had holed up in a clump of boulders just above the bend when he heard the rider below. The horse was weary from the long climb up the steep trail and rocks clattered as its scrabbling hoofs sent them spilling down the slope. He tightened his grip on the rifle stock, starting to take up the trigger slack. He didn't like killing horses but this was necessary, sooooo...

'Judas priest!' He threw the rifle barrel up just as the hammer fell. The shot crashed and echoed through the timber, whining away into the leaden skies. The rider below jumped in the saddle and almost fell, fighting the startled horse.

Birch stood up, automatically levering another shell into the breech. He let the rider get control of the horse, then, as they settled down, he called:

'Just hold it right there! That's it! Now you didn't follow me in here just because of my good looks. So you come on up here, slow an' careful, an' tell me just what the *hell* you think you're doin', Mrs Travis!'

11

Undercover Agent

Cody Travis came round slowly and painfully. It took him several foggy minutes before he remembered how he came to be in an abandoned line shack with two dead men.

But it was only seconds before he realized he had been shot in the head. He could feel the line of soreness under his hair, tightening his scalp, thick and sticky with blood in a shallow groove. His eyelids were sticky, too.

When he moved his left arm – and it *hurt* to do so, that side of his neck being stiff – he almost passed out. Gingerly he felt around the wound area with lightly probing fingers.

The bullet hadn't gone deep. It had torn across the scalp, taking hair and his hat with it as it buried itself somewhere in the flimsy wall. Not that it mattered where the lead was now as long as it wasn't still in him. He dragged himself across to Wrango's war bag with the saddle canteen strapped to the ouside, drank deeply, then soaked his neckerchief well and gently washed away the crusted blood, first from his eyes, then the wound itself. The groove bled a little but soon stopped. He knew he wasn't going to be able to bandage the wound in such an awkward position with what he had but he rinsed out the cloth, squeezed it, soaked it again and held it in place as he edged over to Wrango's body and literally tore the man's shirt off his back.

He twisted it several times, then, grunting with the pain of lifting his arms, placed it over the wadded kerchief and tied it beneath his chin. He had a moment of levity when he tried to picture himself, but then the pain hit again and he clawed at the wall for support.

The cabin was filled with the grey light of an overcast day and he became aware of the hushed sound of light rain falling on the shingle roof. It leaked in a few places and dripped monotonously. Travis, near-exhausted by his efforts, spread out Wrango's bedroll and flopped into it on his back. He banged his head in the process and groaned, almost passing out, even as he heard a horse outside.

He couldn't see the yard properly although the door was partly ajar, jammed that way by Kiley's body. But he heard the creak of saddle leather and boots coming towards the shack. He worked his sixgun free of the holster but his fingers were sticky with blood and he fumbled it. Then a man appeared in the doorway, shapeless in a glistening poncho, holding a cocked sixgun.

Travis continued to try to get his gun up as the man stepped over Kiley's body and strode swiftly towards him.

'Just leave the gun!' the man said sharply. Then he was standing over Travis, water dripping from the battered curl-brim hat. 'Hell, you're in worse shape than me.'

Travis blinked to clear his blurred vision and the man swept off his hat, revealing bandages around his head.

'Pecos,' breathed Travis and then passed out all the way this time.

Big Abe McKinley was still mighty sore and the scabs on his back and face made things awkward in many ways but he was mending fast.

He needed to, for all the things he had planned! He hoped Wrango and Kiley hadn't killed Travis. If they had, he would

167

kill them. There was only one thing he wanted more than to literally break Cody Travis into little pieces but that would come soon now. He had waited all this time – a little longer wouldn't hurt...

He moved stiffly, bare from the waist up, the scabbed wounds plastered with herbs Winona had taught him about all those years ago. They were working, slow but sure, but working. He forced his mind away from memories that wanted to push through to the fore: time enough for that later, too.

First he would take care of Travis and if he could do it before the man had time to send information back to the Cattlemen's Association, then that would be a bonus.

'Where the hell are they?' he muttered aloud.

Stew Hagen, passing within earshot at that moment, stopped, glanced up at the trail that led to the rim of the canyon. The mavericks herded into the far end milled restlessly and bawled but they would be bawling their way along the back trails to Butte before long.

'Mebbe Travis got Wrango and Kiley, Abe,' he opined and wished he'd kept his mouth shut, the way McKinley glared at him. 'Well – I'm still recallin' the way he gunned down Chuck Farraday–'

'You better be wrong!'

'Rain might've held 'em up...'

'Aw, shut up, Stew!'

'Whatever you say, Abe. We're ready to head 'em up an' move 'em out any time you say.' He indicated the penned mavericks.

'Goddamnit! We oughta be drivin' right now, but the way it looks it'll have to be tomorrow. Hey! What was that? You see movement up there?'

Hagen had: just within the timberline there was a flash of colour. Like a roan horse – but he knew neither Kiley nor Wrango were riding a roan. His hand was already resting on his gun butt when he saw the riders, checked the exclamation that rose to his lips and looked sharply at Abe.

'Now, what the hell...!' the big man breathed as a man and a woman appeared on the rim. 'Lew Birch and – *smoke me!* Mrs Uppity Abby Travis!' Suddenly a wide, tight smile split his battered face. 'Well, now, this might be even better than her old man comin' in!'

Lew Birch lifted a hand and motioned to the woman to ride ahead of him down the steep trail that dropped into the canyon.

It was then that Stew Hagen noticed

Abby's hands were roped to the saddlehorn.

'Just what did Stedmann say in his letter about the Association sendin' in an undercover agent, Abe?'

Lew Birch sipped his mug of powerfully strong coffee, leaning his rheumaticky hips against a boulder near the cook-fire the rustlers had built outside the lean-to.

Abby Travis was standing nearby, rubbing her rope reddened wrists, the skin broken in a couple of places. It had been a rough ride up here. Her vest and blouse were torn from the brush and her denim trousers were smeared with mud. The ends of her hair were wet from the rain and her narrow-brimmed hat was soggy and shapeless. She looked rather pathetic standing there under the scrutiny of Big Abe McKinley and his rustlers.

Abe kept his gaze on her as he answered Birch's question about the undercover agent.

'Said he was pretty sure the agent they'd hired was Travis.'

Birch nodded. 'He was right.'

'Hell, I *know* that!' snapped Abe but as he made to continue, Lew Birch interrupted him.

'No, Abe – not *Cody* Travis. *Her!*'

The rustlers gaped and Abe frowned, slowly swivelled his eyes to Abby who, although pale and tense, held his gaze unwaveringly.

'The hell you say!'

Birch nodded, sipping his coffee again, grimacing.

'This is God-awful java! She's the one, Abe. Before she married Cody, her name was Roth.'

'So?'

'Ross's real name. Her brother. A Yellowstone Park ranger before turnin' range detective for the Association. We might've learned more if Wrango hadn't pushed him off the rim.'

'So Wrango murdered my brother!' breathed Abby. 'I hope Cody's killed him, but if he hasn't, I surely will!' She saw the smirk on McKinley's face and added hotly: 'And don't for one minute think I'm not capable of it. I've never been afraid of getting a little blood on my hands!'

Birch smiled crookedly, jerking his head in her direction.

'Full of spunk! Had hell's own job gettin' her to admit she was Dysart's agent. Told me she got the news about Ross's death just before she married Cody. She postponed the weddin', went straight to Dysart and did a deal with him. Make Cody manager of Thistle and she'd tag along as an undercover agent for the Association. No one would suspect her. She had plenty motivation: Ross was her *twin* brother and twins are a lot closer than normal brothers and sisters. She was followin' me, hopin' I'd lead her to Ross's killer.'

'And whoever gave the order for Michael's murder!'

Abe smiled at her. 'Wrango did it on the spur of the moment – made a whole heap of trouble, too. We had to rig things to make Ross's death look accidental. Thanks to Lew we managed it, but even he weren't pleased about it.'

'Perhaps you didn't pay him enough!' Abby snapped and Birch flinched under her gaze.

Abe laughed. 'You hit Lew where it hurts, Abby! He never was happy takin' money from us, but he's too old for any other job now, got no savin's, no family to take care of him in his old age, so he figured he might's well pocket a leetle graft to ease him through his last few years…'

'Forget me, Abe. What're you goin' to do

about her?' *He was sorry he'd brought her along now. Maybe too late…*

Abe widened his grin, not even noticing that he started a couple of sores bleeding.

'Now, thinkin' about that is gonna gimme a mighty pleasant night, Lew. By the by, just what're you doin' up this way?'

'I came to get Wrango. He beat Jack Woodring to death. Figured if I took in the man who did it, then there'd be less chance of a marshal bein' sent in. Told you they're crackin' down on lawlessness now that Montana's about to be admitted to the Union. An' once they start pokin' around, you never know what they'll turn up.'

'Like how your bank balance is growin' faster'n you can earn the money that goes into it!' Abe said and quickly held up a hand as Birch started to speak angrily. 'This is the last lot of mavericks, anyway.'

Birch drew down a deep breath and nodded.

'So I'll be off the payroll. OK by me – I've had a bellyful after all this time, but – tell me somethin', Abe: all them mavericks you rustled and sold – none of you seem to've gotten rich. The town businessmen are always bitchin' about Thistle hands spendin' so little. So what's been the point of it all?'

Abe McKinley was sober now, his dark eyes narrowed.

'My boys only got their wages to draw on and most of 'em owe me money. There's a pool of the *dinero* earned from the mavericks. It'll be paid out to the survivors later – and the fewer there are, the bigger the share for each.'

'Survivors?' echoed a puzzled Lew.

Abe shrugged. 'Those still alive after we collect on the last lot of mavericks, and do one final chore. I control the pool. No one else can get to the money, so they all work to make sure *I* survive, no matter what.'

'I've heard of such arrangements. You get the biggest share, of course.'

McKinley shook his head, watching the attentive woman now.

'Not me. I get no more than a few bucks for expenses. The rest goes to buy guns.'

Birch sat down on the rock, shaking his head, bewildered. But Big Abe kept his gaze on Abby who was frowning, not understanding. He smiled crookedly.

'You heard of a place called Silver Bow? There was a massacre there.'

Birch stiffened and Abby spoke slowly.

'Ye-es – three years ago, wasn't it? The army decided to put an end to the Indian uprisings here and made a series of punitive raids, wiping out the renegades, village by village–'

'Not *just* the renegades!' roared Abe, making Abby jump, drawing all attention to himself. His big fists were curled up at his sides. 'No – they didn't just stick to killin' a few wild bucks, they hit all the villages, killed everyone, old people, women, kids–'

'But – Silver Bow!' Abby said, suddenly remembering. 'That wasn't the army! Their resources were stretched to the limit so they agreed to civilians forming their own raiding parties, and to turn a blind eye to whatever, and however, blood was spilled. Just in an all-out effort to end the slaughter of settlers and raids on army posts and wagon trains. They were desperate, and the settlers were demanding that something be done.'

Abe was looking at her closely now. Breath hissed audibly through his nostrils. 'You got that part right, Abby. The goddamn civilian raidin' parties were worse than the soldiers. And Silver Bow, up there on the Big Hole River, was a sittin' duck when they decided to hit it just before dawn while everyone was sleepin'...' For a fraction of a second his voice faltered, then firmed again, hard with something that Abby recognized with surprise as absolute hatred. '...and they massacred the entire village. There were no warriors there – they were hidin' in the hills from the army. Most still are, come to that. No, there were just old folks, some young women, kids. Among them was a half-breed gal only eighteen years old with a baby at her breast...' He paused a long moment now as he said in a hushed voice, 'She was visitin' her Indian mother, showin' off the kid. Her name was Winona – and she was my wife. The kid was my son.'

There was a strange hush in the canyon and it seemed to drag on for ever until Abe McKinley, his once-handsome face reflecting the hatred he felt, added in a flat, dead voice:

'Every one of those civilian raiders at Silver Bow were from Hatfield – except for a couple dozen cowboys from Thistle and Horseshoe, led by Jock Dysart and Herb Anders.'

'And that's why you're rustlin' their cows!' said Lew Birch.

'Hell, I aimed to keep on doin' it, ruin the sons of bitches, take all their hopes away from them like they took mine at Silver Bow! But now there's enough to buy guns.'

'What're you going to do with them?'

Abby asked quietly.

Abe glared, then smiled crookedly.

'Happen to know where a bunch of renegade bucks are holed up. The leader is kin of Winona's. The army thinks they've beat 'em but they're just waitin' their chance. And I aim to give it to 'em.'

'You're actually going to arm renegade Indians?' Abby asked, aghast. 'With modern firearms?'

Even some of the rustlers stirred uncomfortably.

'They ain't forgot the massacre at Silver Bow, or that it was men from Hatfield done it. I'm just givin' 'em a chance to square things, let them bastards see what it's like to watch *their* families butchered in front of 'em … all the time knowin' that no matter what they do, *they*'re gonna die, too – hard and screamin'!'

'You're plumb loco!' said Lew Birch. 'They'll never stop at Hatfield! They'll sweep right through this valley, slaughterin' every white they come across.'

'Who the hell cares?' McKinley said bitterly and Abby was startled to see his eyes were moist. 'They took the only woman I ever loved away from me, split her from scalp to crotch with an axe, beat my son's brains out against a tree. You think I give a shit what happens to the people who done that?'

'The Indians might turn on you, too, once their bloodlust is up!' warned Abby, shaken by Big Abe's passion and his story.

He placed his big hands on his hips and his wild eyes bored into hers.

'So...? You really think I care what happens to me? Hell, I died three years ago – I just haven't bothered to lie down yet, is all!'

12

Vengeance is Mine

'Don't reckon you oughta even think about ridin' boss,' Pecos said worriedly as Travis stood slowly and took a few shaky steps around the line shack. 'You don't look so good and you're swayin' like a willow in the wind.'

'I'm dizzy,' Travis admitted, putting a hand out to the wall. 'But I'll be OK in a few minutes.'

'But it's one helluva ride to that canyon, if it's the one I'm thinkin' of.'

Pecos had once seen Stew Hagen and Wrango coming out of the hills when they had been supposedly clearing weed and silt away from the dam's headgates, miles in the other direction. Curious, Pecos, accompanied by Jack Woodring at the time, had left the rounded-up cows they were bringing in and followed the trail left by Hagen and Wrango once the men were out of sight. It had been raining lightly and the tracks were easy to read.

They had heard the distant bawling of cows, knowing by the sound they were young mavericks penned for the first time in their lives. Then they had seen Abe McKinley ride on to the rim, coming up a trail they couldn't see from their position, but certain-sure it had to lead out of a hidden canyon. He'd reined aside to allow three Indians to drive four cows past, waving them off in friendly manner.

Neither cowboy wanted to tangle with Big Abe and although they figured something shady was going on, they simply got out of there and kept their mouths shut. Giving Indians a little beef was common enough with ranchers: it saved raids on their herds and didn't cost much in the long run if it prevented trouble with the wild-eyed bucks who still roamed this neck of the woods. Come to that, wide-looping a few of the boss's mavericks wasn't exactly unknown, either.

Pecos had bandaged Travis's head wound, using strips torn from a sheet in Wrango's bedroll. It looked way better than the crude job Travis had done on himself. Not that the wound felt any better, mind – it hurt like hell and his head felt as if it had been laid open with a tomahawk.

It was when Travis said he felt well enough to ride that Pecos told him about what he and Jack Woodring had seen at the hidden canyon. Travis recalled how the Indians had backed off from the buckboard on the way to the ranch when they had seen the thistle painted on the side; they collected free beef, and in return gave Thistle safe passage.

'Let's go alooking while we've still got enough light,' he said. 'This gets more interesting by the minute.'

That was when Pecos told Travis he didn't think he should try to sit a saddle.

'Be better goin' back to the ranch,' the Texan added.

'Why? You said Abby hadn't come back from town by the time you left, so I can't expect any better treatment for the wound than what you've given me – which is fine. So get your gear, Pecos, we're moving out.'

'Hell, I only come to tell you about Jack!'

'You told me, now it's time to do something about it. I've got a headache a mustang couldn't jump over and I'm in no mood for more talk...'

So that was it.

Anyway, Pecos figured he wouldn't mind having a crack at these rustlers: Wrango and

Kiley were dead, but there were still Stew Hagen, Southpaw, Patchett, Race Satterfield and – his belly gave a bit of a lurch when he thought about Abe McKinley, but the man had to be dealt with – there was no way out of it.

While Travis was stumbling about outside calling his smoky-grey mount, Pecos scrawled a note with a lump of charcoal on a piece of Wrango's sheet, giving a rough direction. Just in case Bud Corey came up here looking for Travis. Might be they would need a hand if they did actually find the canyon.

But once mounted, Pecos shook his head worriedly when he saw the way Cody Travis was slumped in his saddle. He looked about ready to topple off and the damn horse was only travelling at walking-pace.

This was going to be some ride, he allowed silently, moving close alongside Travis's mount.

By now it seemed likely that Wrango and Kiley weren't going to return to the rustlers' canyon. Admitting it to himself didn't make Abe McKinley any happier.

'That son of a bitch, Travis!' he griped within hearing of Abby who had been roped to one of the uprights of the lean-to. She was wet from the rain that had fallen earlier and shivered a little.

'There's more to Cody than you think, isn't there?' she told Abe with a sly satisfaction at seeing the worry on his face. 'He'll get you in the end, Abe, make no mistake about it.'

He strode across, grabbed her by the jaw with one of his big hands and squeezed until tears of pain filled her eyes. Then, abruptly, he kissed her on the puckered lips and laughed harshly, thrusting her back roughly as far as her bonds would allow.

'Maybe you won't be around to see one way or t'other!'

'Oh! And I thought you'd be smart enough to keep me for something to bargain with!'

He curled a lip. 'Yeah, well, could be...'

'Then again,' she said, smiling crookedly although it hurt, 'Cody may not want to bargain. You see, I haven't played very square with Cody. I meant to, but – well, he seemed to be doing fine and I didn't want to give him any kind of worry that might – make him take a drink again.'

'Once a drunk, always a drunk,' McKinley told her sourly, smugly.

'Cody beat it once and he could do it

again if he had to. But it's a – a long battle. I helped him before but I'm not sure…' She paused before putting the thought into words, then looked at him defiantly. 'I'm not sure I'm going to come out of this alive.'

'Want me to tell you?' he asked.

She held his jeering gaze. 'I made a vow that I would avenge my brother's death and I *will* do that, whatever it costs. But I love Cody and I'd like a chance to make it up to him for – using him the way I have.'

'You're sayin' Travis don't know you work for the Association?' asked Lew Birch suddenly. He had come up in time to hear Abby's speech and he paused now in packing his pipe.

'That's right, Sheriff. I only told you because I saw a chance that you'd bring me to this hideout where I would be close enough to reach the men who ordered Michael killed.'

Birch blew out his leathery lips.

'You've got some guts, lady. Ain't she, Abe?'

McKinley gave that crooked smile again, winked at her.

'I'll kill anyone who stands between me and what I want, now that I'm this close to gettin' it – and that includes you.'

'Cody'll stop you!' she told him confidently, enjoying the way her words wiped the smile off his scarred face.

'He's likely dead already. Wrango an' Kiley weren't no cream-puffs.'

'But they're not here, are they? And you're already talking about them in the past tense!'

Abe shrugged. 'Sure, Travis might've nailed 'em. But if he has, I bet he's picked up a dose of lead poisonin', too! Like I said, he weren't goin' up agin a couple amateurs!'

It was Abby's turn to lose her smile.

Satterfield and the other rustlers were growing restless and Stew Hagen sauntered over to Abe.

'When're we gonna move them cows, Abe? Me and the boys're kinda jumpy.'

'Might's well wait overnight now.' McKinley growled. 'Stedmann'll hold up till we get there. He knows this is the last lot.'

'Yeah, but,' Hagen moved from one foot to the other. 'Well, fact is, Abe, we don't like not knowin' where Travis is. He might bring Corey and the rest lookin' for us.'

'He don't know about this place...' Abe paused, looked across at Abby. She had been released by Southpaw and was now hunkering down by the fire, reheating the pot of stew for a meal. 'Or does he...?'

He crossed quickly to where she was preparing vegetables to add, seized a handful of her hair and flung her sprawling on the ground.

Lew Birch tensed, taking his pipe from his mouth, transferring it from his right to his left hand. His hard eyes narrowed as Abe towered over the woman who looked up at him, alarm showing on her face.

'Travis know about this place?' he snapped.

'Of course,' she lied easily, sensing some small advantage here. 'He saw Stew Hagen coming out of these hills one day and back-trailed him.'

Abe glared at Stew who swallowed and shook his head swiftly. 'Ain't true, Abe! No one never seen me up this way. I always looked, covered my trail in any case. She's lyin'.'

McKinley nodded slowly. 'Yeah, reckon she is. Otherwise she wouldn't've had to use Lew to bring her here.'

'*I* didn't know about this place,' Abby said easily. 'But Cody did. In fact, he warned me to stay away from this area.'

Big Abe swore, not knowing whether to

believe her or not now. He leaned down and slapped her hard across the face, making her hair fly.

'Bitch! Just get that grub ready!'

Lew Birch helped the dazed woman to her feet.

She blinked back tears of pain and put a hand to her face where Abe's finger marks showed in red welts outlined in white. The sheriff steadied her, looking at the big man.

'No need for that, Abe,' the lawman said quietly.

'Who the hell asked you? Anyways, what're you still doin' here? You ain't needed no more.'

Birch flushed, glancing sidelong at the woman. 'I'm owed money.'

'You'll get it after Stedmann pays us for the mavericks.'

'Reckon I'd like to see it now if you don't mind. You haven't included me in that "pool", I'll bet.'

'I said you'll get paid,' McKinley said dangerously. 'Don't push your luck, Lew!'

'My luck's never been good. I have to give it a nudge along now and again.'

Big Abe sighed. 'I ever tried to cheat you?'

'Not that I know of. But you needed me before. Now you say you don't.'

The big man glared, ran a hand through his hair.

'You're beginnin' to bother me, Lew. Mebbe you'd like to ride along just to make sure you get your share...?'

Birch hesitated, then nodded. 'Yeah, well, that seems like a good notion. But the girl has to be–'

McKinley's big hand almost swallowed the Colt that seemed to spring into it from his holster. Lew Birch reacted pretty fast for a man so out of shape and plagued by rheumatics: he threw himself aside, reaching for his own gun, but a blind man could see he was going to be way too slow.

Desperately, Abby shoved Abe hard just as he fired but Birch was spun violently, staggering off balance, causing Abe to miss with his next shot. McKinley back-handed the girl, knocking her sprawling, jumped back as Lew Birch got off a shot just as he sprawled on the ground. Abe triggered again and Birch slammed back, wrenching on to one side, his gun falling from fingers too weak to hold it any longer.

Abby, pale now, gathered herself and crabbed swiftly over to the still lawman. She glanced down at his blood-splotched shirt, and looked quickly over her shoulder at the towering McKinley. 'You murderer! You didn't have to kill him!'

'Says who?' Abe growled, his eye bright with the excitement of action and death. He began to reload his sixgun. 'I do what I want, ain't no *have to* about it! An' I sure don't need your permission. Stew, shove the old coot over the edge of that gully yonder.'

Abby, white with anger, threw herself across the lawman's hunched body.

'*No!* Damn you, Abe McKinley! He was a good man, even if a little weak! He deserves better!'

'Aw, gee, you're makin' me feel real bad. I think I'm gonna cry!'

'You – you have no respect for anyone!' she snapped, breasts heaving with her emotion. 'Living or dead! I – I'll just roll him in his blanket and we'll give him a decent burial when Cody comes!'

For a chilling moment Abby thought she had gone too far and that Abe was going to kill her, too. But he curled a lip and turned away, stomping off.

'Do what you like. And hurry up with that stew!' He leered over his shoulder at her. 'Killin' always spices up my appetite!'

Laughing, in a good mood now, he walked away, gesturing for Stew Hagen to follow.

189

The man hesitated but then shrugged and went towards the lean-to where the others waited. They watched while Abby strained and panted to wrap Lew Birch's body loosely in the lawman's blanket which she fetched from his bedroll.

She kept moving around and around, folding in a corner here, tucking in a flap there, sweating, but determined to give the old lawman some semblance of dignity in death.

When she returned to the bubbling stew, the savoury smell had the men calling her to hurry it up – they were hungry.

'I just have to add a few spices and it'll be ready,' she called, her back to them as she tipped in some chili powder and salt from a ragged square of paper. She stirred it in well with a long wooden spoon and tasted a little. She turned and smiled at the men. 'One hearty stew coming up...'

The meal went well, all the men coming back for seconds. Abe said to make sure there was enough left for a third plate, then looked hard at her.

'You ain't eatin'.'

Her face sobered. 'You spoiled my appetite. Anyway I'm worried about Cody now.'

The big man grinned. 'Mebbe you should

start worryin' about yourself a little more.'

Her teeth tugged at her lower lip and she spoke in a hushed voice. 'Perhaps I should...'

'Damn right,' Abe told her, starting to fill his platter for the third time. 'You won't fight me off this time.'

Then there came a crash of gunfire from the far end of the canyon.

It was quickly followed by the bawling of cattle and moments later they heard the splintering of the rail fence and three hundred panic-stricken, wild-eyed critters came surging down the canyon towards the rustler's camp.

'*Stampede!*' bawled Race Satterfield, unnecessarily.

Travis seemed to improve as Pecos led the way through the rugged hills and angled in towards where he believed the hidden canyon to be.

The wounded man swayed as he clung to the saddle horn with one hand, the other with the reins wrapped tightly about it. Apart from occasional dizziness and intermittent blurred vision, Cody felt pretty good – better than he had a right to expect. The headache was a damn nuisance but he could stand it – that and a lot more if he had to.

They were drawing close now and he didn't aim to give up. Jack Woodring had been avenged but there was still Abe McKinley and the others to account for. If it cost Travis a little blood and hide to do it, well, that went with the job– *Ride for the brand,* had always been his creed.

There were gusting showers of light rain but the trail wasn't as muddy as Pecos had feared. He had his bearings now, having cut into these hills at just about the same angle as months previously when he and Jack had spotted McKinley and those Indians with the steers. He was glad Wrango and Kiley were dead, but he knew the real killer of his sidekick was Abe McKinley: he was the one who would have given the orders for the beating.

'You still OK back there, Cody?' he called over his shoulder.

'Doing OK.' Cody sounded a little breathless and he looked pale, squinted a lot, but there was an air of stubbornness and determination about him and Pecos knew he was going to make it.

Somehow.

Then Pecos picked up one of the landmarks that told him they were drawing close.

'Eyes up, Cody! Won't be long now!'

Travis looked around him. 'This isn't the place where Abby and me saw Stew Hagen.'

'Well, up there's where me and Jack seen Big Abe and them Injuns.' He pointed through the trees swaying in the damp wind.

Cody frowned. 'We must be coming in from a different direction.'

'Sure: we're well to the south and west now. We had to cut down from that line shack, you know, and that's on Horseshoe land.'

Travis had it figured then. They were headed in the right direction, only the point he was looking for was more northerly.

'We must be coming in from the back of the canyon.'

'Dunno – but I'll swear on a stack of Bibles this'll take us in to where we want to go.'

Cody signed for Pecos to continue, took out his sixgun and checked the loads, did the same with his Winchester.

One way or another, this was going to end today!

There were deep shadows cast by the ridges as they made their way downslope through brush and light timber.

Pecos figured this was behind the high trail where he and Jack Woodring had seen McKinley and he was proved right within minutes of hitting the bottom.

On the way down they heard what could have been a couple of gunshots, but the bawling of cattle echoing on the rain-heavy air made them uncertain.

'Think that was gunfire?' Pecos asked, tensed now.

Travis didn't reply, searching for some kind of entrance. He pointed.

'Where that shadow line suddenly breaks and then continues, Pecos! Looks like a narrow cutting. If it is, that's our way in.'

He was right. They approached with rifles unsheathed and loaded, thumbs on hammer spurs, ready to cock for the first shot. A gust of warmer air blew out of the canyon, bringing the odour of cattledung and hides with it – and also a savoury smell of cooking meat.

'Gonna eat well by the smell of that,' opined Pecos as they eased into the cutting.

'Kind of hungry myself,' Travis said absently, alert now.

The entrance was narrow, room for no more than three riders abreast, but then it widened gradually into the canyon beyond. There was a rail fence across the inner end of the cutting, keeping the mavericks from breaking out this way.

The cattle were restless, moved away when they saw the two riders, but another fence across the canyon kept them penned up. Then they saw the rustlers' camp, the light uncertain because of the deep shadow cast by the canyon wall, but they could make out the lean-to and several people moving about. Abe McKinley's big form was the only one they could definitely recognize. The rest were blurred as they squatted near a camp-fire, apparently eating.

'That camp's on the flat,' Travis said slowly. 'Looks like six, seven men there.'

Pecos, sweating now, licked his lips.

'Yeah, that's the count I get. Odds're a mite bigger than I figured on.'

'So we'll cut 'em down.'

Cody glanced at Pecos, saw the Texan was willing enough but there were obvious signs that the man would rather be someplace else.

Well, hell, so would Cody, if he was honest about it, but this was something that had to be done.

There could be no turning back at this point...

With a few grunts he dismounted and climbed up on to the short fence at the inner edge of the cutting, straining to see across the backs of the cows but making sure he wasn't high enough to be seen by those inside the canyon.

Travis was moving about more comfortably now, his voice stronger.

'That long fence on the camp side doesn't look too strong. See how the posts lean outwards from the cows pushing against them? They try a little harder, they'll flatten that fence.'

'I guess rustlers ain't known for workin' any harder'n they have to. That fence has been up a couple years at least. You got a small stampede in mind by any chance?'

Travis smiled thinly. 'They seem to be eating right now, so...?'

'Worth a try!' Pecos was on edge: shoot-outs with murderous rustlers were not part of the usual working day for him, although he had done his part for whatever brand he had been working for when called upon. 'Ready when you are, Cody!'

Travis lifted his rifle and fired three fast shots into the air. Pecos fired twice into the herd, planting his lead amongst the feet of the cows.

They reared and bawled and lunged, crushing those at the front hard against the fence, instinctively moving away from the two riders who were doing the shooting. The fence posts tilted and fibres cracked. The pressure increased as panic swept through the young cows. The fence toppled with a volley of splintering sounds and then the herd was surging through the gap, bawling and kicking and tossing their heads as they started to run without much co-ordination.

The raiders were mounted again now, thankful for the recent rain, for there wasn't much dust kicked up from the damp ground, and, by standing in the stirrups, they could see the movements of the rustlers in the camp. Two looked to be doubled-up, vomiting. Others were running in every direction, several trying to get up the slope to the corrals and their mounts. They appeared to be stumbling a lot, almost staggering.

Travis could make out the giant figure of Abe McKinley. The man lurched as he shouted orders, gun in hand. He was obviously unsteady on his feet. Drunk, maybe...?

The herd thundered down on the camp.

The mavericks might be young but they were in the grip of the stampede terror and every bit as dangerous as a herd of long-horns. Their hoofs were just as sharp and destructive and their rolling eyes were dulled with the driving, mindless and collective horror that seemed to be built into every bovine creature, communicating effortlessly from one to another.

Abe had rallied most of his men and they were shooting at the cows now. Two men reached their mounts and kicked down some of the corral rails. They clambered aboard clumsily, one man falling, trying again, finally successful. They rode bareback towards the far exit of the canyon.

Travis threw up his rifle, sighted fast, led his target and squeezed off a shot. Before he saw the rider jerk and spill from the racing horse – now followed by the other mounts fleeing from the corrals – he had another cartridge levered into the chamber. He started to swing the rifle to the second rider but Pecos' shot brought down both horse and man. Dazed, the man started up, looking around him stupidly – and then the herd swept in to and over him. If he screamed it was lost in the thunder of the cows.

Travis was standing in the stirrups, swinging his rifle, searching for Big Abe McKinley. The man was unmistakable and had a rifle now, shooting at Travis and Pecos. Cody fired and his shot kicked mud over Abe's boots. Then Abe's rifle jammed. He flung it aside and lunged for someone who was crouched over, trying to drag what looked like a blanket-roll out of the path of the stampede.

Travis was startled to see McKinley sweep up the man in one arm and suddenly hold him high and effortlessly above his head. He was looking towards Travis, mouth working, but Cody couldn't make out what he was saying.

Then he felt the sick lurch in his belly as he recognized Abe's burden. *'Oh, Christ! It's Abby!'*

Abe had to move as the cows spread out more now, a stream of them lifting up the small slope towards the lean-to, scattering the cooking-fire. He ran with long strides, stumbling but still carrying the struggling woman. On a small projecting ledge he stopped, turned to look back towards Travis and Pecos and bared white teeth in a vicious grin.

'No!' yelled Travis.

199

But he was too late. McKinley hurled Abby towards the stampede and she disappeared from sight, hidden by the heaving backs of the jostling herd.

At the same time, Abe McKinley staggered back so violently that Travis thought Pecos had shot him. But Pecos was shooting in the opposite direction.

Travis was too sickened to care about anything but Abby. With a sudden roar he plunged his protesting mount into the edge of the stampede. It was thinning out now at this side and he raked the horse's flanks cruelly with his spurs, riding back and forth, failing to find Abby. Then he saw Abe McKinley...

He kicked cows aside as they instinctively nudged his mount with their heads and shoulders, shot one animal that refused to get out of his way. His head was roaring. His vision seemed sharper than ever as he frantically sought Abe.

The big man was running up the slope to where three mounts were still cornered in the corral, afraid to venture out into the stampede. Abe was limping and faltering but he had a gun in his hand and he turned and triggered twice at Travis who was breaking out of the herd now. He saw Stew

Hagen, bloody, stumbling with one hand held to his chest and then Pecos' rifle cracked and Hagen went down. Southpaw was already sprawled on the ground. A white-faced Race Satterfield lunged at Travis, trying to unseat him, wanting the sweating mount. Cody slammed him across the head with his rifle barrel and his horse stumbled as Race tangled in its legs.

Free again, Travis fired the rifle one-handed as Patchett, on one knee, blood on his neck, brought up his gun. The man went down as if kicked, head snapping back.

Cody had eyes only for Abe McKinley, saw the man running into the corrals, his speed frightening the trio of mounts even more. They dodged his roaring lunges, two escaping past him, almost colliding with Travis as he spurred in and without slackening speed, rammed his mount full-tilt into McKinley. Abe was hurled, violently spinning, back two yards.

Even as the giant went down, Travis saw the bloodstains showing low down on his right side. Abe hit hard, skidded, rolled, and the remaining mount stepped on him as it lunged for the corral gate, no longer afraid to move as the last of the herd rumbled by on its way to the canyon's exit.

Travis dismounted and flung his rifle aside: it was empty now. As he drew his sixgun he was surprised to see Abe getting to his feet, face streaked with blood, left arm dangling uselessly, a section of white bone protruding from the forearm. It must have been enormously painful but the giant rustler appeared to ignore it. Standing with boots spread, swaying, blood dripping from his wounds, he smiled at Travis.

'I – took her – from you. I – won!' he gasped.

'Take that thought with you to hell!' Travis gritted and lifted the sixgun, as a voice called,

'Cody! She's still alive!'

He whirled, head spinning again, stared in disbelief as he saw Pecos standing beside a battered-looking Lew Birch who was on one knee, supporting Abby in his arms. Travis only had time to see patches of blood and dirt on her and then there was a massive roar like a grizzly behind him and he turned to find Abe McKinley only a yard from him and advancing like a runaway train, reaching for him with his right hand. Travis swayed to one side but the fingers gripped his throat and he felt the bones starting to crush in his neck as Big Abe lifted him clear of the ground, teeth bared in a rictus of hate.

Travis rammed the muzzle of his sixgun against those white teeth and dropped the hammer. Abe staggered back, and Travis fell, breath rasping into his lungs. He saw the giant collapse, one side of his face torn off as he spread out on the ground...

Travis fell to his knees, let his sixgun fall and crawled down the slope to where Abby and the others waited.

It looked as though she had only been touched by the edge of the stampede. She had been trampled only a little, thanks to Lew Birch's wounding Abe McKinley just as the man hurled Abby from him. Even so she had one arm broken, and maybe a rib or two, a leg badly hoof-cut and a bump on her head above her right eye. But through the blood and dirt she smiled weakly at him and groped for him with her right hand.

He found it and held it, glanced at the grey-faced sheriff.

'Guess you saved Abby by shooting Abe just as he threw her.'

Birch nodded, two patches of blood on his shirt.

'Well, she saved my life. Abe shot me and she made him believe I was dead, wrapped me in my blanket – with my sixgun… Had a helluva job kickin' free, but I made it in time, I guess.'

'That you did,' Travis said feelingly.

'What was wrong with all them rustlers?' Pecos asked abruptly. 'They was a-staggerin' all over the place. I even saw some vomitin'. Didn't seem to know what they was doin'.'

'I – put a drug in the – stew,' gasped Abby. 'Brought it with me from the doctor's – quite powerful emetic.'

Travis gently pushed matted hair back from Abby's pale face.

'The odds were pretty big against us, even with the stampede. Putting those rustlers in a bind like that likely saved our necks…'

'Cody – I – I – have a lot of – explaining to do – I'm sorry I – had to – use you the way I did…'

'That can wait. We'll get you patched up and back to the ranch.' Cody looked at Birch. 'You, too, Lew. You gonna stick around for a spell?'

The old sheriff hesitated.

'Well, you know, I just might do that now. Wasn't aimin' to, but – I figure I can finish my career with a little more pride and respect now. Thanks to you and your woman, Cody.'

Cody Travis smiled wearily, looking fondly at Abby. 'Yeah. She sure is something, isn't she?'

The publishers hope that this book has given you enjoyable reading. Large Print Books are especially designed to be as easy to see and hold as possible. If you wish a complete list of our books please ask at your local library or write directly to:

Dales Large Print Books
Magna House, Long Preston,
Skipton, North Yorkshire.
BD23 4ND

This Large Print Book, for people
who cannot read normal print,
is published under the auspices of

THE ULVERSCROFT FOUNDATION

... we hope you have enjoyed this book.
Please think for a moment about those
who have worse eyesight than you ...
and are unable to even read or enjoy
Large Print without great difficulty.

You can help them by sending a
donation, large or small, to:

**The Ulverscroft Foundation,
1, The Green, Bradgate Road,
Anstey, Leicestershire, LE7 7FU,
England.**
or request a copy of our brochure for
more details.

The Foundation will use all donations
to assist those people who are visually
impaired and need special attention
with medical research, diagnosis
and treatment.

Thank you very much for your help.